MORLEY LIBRARY
184 PHELPS STREET
PAINESVILLE, OHIO 44077
(440) 352-3383

Religion and World Conflict

Religion and World Conflict

Other titles in the World History series

The Age of Colonialism
Ancient Greece
The Byzantine Empire
The Early Middle Ages
Elizabethan England
The Late Middle Ages
The Nuremberg Trials
The Relocation of the North American Indian
The Roman Empire
The Roman Republic

Religion and World Conflict

Ted Hodges

LUCENT BOOKS
An imprint of Thomson Gale, a part of The Thomson Corporation

THOMSON
GALE

Detroit • New York • San Francisco • San Diego • New Haven, Conn. • Waterville, Maine • London • Munich

© 2006 Thomson Gale, a part of The Thomson Corporation.

Thomson and Star Logo are trademarks and Gale and Lucent Books are registered trademarks used herein under license.

For more information, contact
Lucent Books
27500 Drake Rd.
Farmington Hills, MI 48331-3535
Or you can visit our Internet site at http://www.gale.com

ALL RIGHTS RESERVED.
No part of this work covered by the copyright hereon may be reproduced or used in any form or by any means—graphic, electronic, or mechanical, including photocopying, recording, taping, Web distribution or information storage retrieval systems—without the written permission of the publisher.

Every effort has been made to trace the owners of copyrighted material.

LIBRARY OF CONGRESS CATALOGING-IN-PUBLICATION DATA

Hodges, Ted.
 Religion and world conflict / by Ted Hodges.
     p. cm. -- (World history)
 Includes bibliographical references and index.
 ISBN 13: 978-1-59018-642-8 (hardcover : alk. paper)
 ISBN 10: 1-59018-642-7 (hardcover : alk. paper)
 1. Violence--Religious aspects—Juvenile literature. 2.Religion and international affairs—Juvenile literature. 3. War--Religious aspects—Juvenile literature. I. Title.
 BL65.V55H63 2007
 201'.7273--dc22
                                                                    2006019391

Printed in the United States of America

Contents

Foreword	8
Important Dates in Religious World Conflict	10
Introduction:	
Killing in God's Name	12
Chapter One:	
Warfare Driven by Fundamentalist Beliefs	19
Chapter Two:	
Holy Wars for Territory or Political Power	35
Chapter Three:	
Religious Hatred and Revenge	48
Chapter Four:	
Warfare Among Members of the Same Faith	63
Chapter Five:	
Terrorism in the Name of Religion	77
Notes	93
For Further Information	95
Index	97
Picture Credits	103
About the Author	104

Foreword

Each year, on the first day of school, nearly every history teacher faces the task of explaining why his or her students should study history. Many reasons have been given. One is that lessons exist in the past from which contemporary society can benefit and learn. Another is that exploration of the past allows us to see the origins of our customs, ideas, and institutions. Concepts such as democracy, ethnic conflict, or even things as trivial as fashion or mores, have historical roots.

Reasons such as these impress few students, however. If anything, these explanations seem remote and dull to young minds. Yet history is anything but dull. And therein lies what is perhaps the most compelling reason for studying history: History is filled with great stories. The classic themes of literature and drama—love and sacrifice, hatred and revenge, injustice and betrayal, adversity and overcoming adversity—fill the pages of history books, feeding the imagination as well as any of the great works of fiction do.

The story of the Children's Crusade, for example, is one of the most tragic in history. In 1212 Crusader fever hit Europe. A call went out from the pope that all good Christians should journey to Jerusalem to drive out the hated Muslims and return the city to Christian control. Heeding the call, thousands of children made the journey. Parents bravely allowed many children to go, and entire communities were inspired by the faith of these small Crusaders. Unfortunately, many boarded ships captained by slave traders, who enthusiastically sold the children into slavery as soon as they arrived at their destination. Thousands died from disease, exposure, and starvation on the long march across Europe to the Mediterranean Sea. Others perished at sea.

Another story, from a modern and more familiar place, offers a soul-wrenching view of personal humiliation but also the ability to rise above it. Hatsuye Egami was one of 110,000 Japanese Americans sent to internment camps during World War II. "Since yesterday we Japanese have ceased to be human beings," he wrote in his diary. "We are numbers. We are no longer Egamis, but the number 23324. A tag with that number is on every trunk, suitcase and bag. Tags, also, on our breasts." Despite such dehumanizing treatment, most internees worked hard to control their bitterness. They created workable communities inside the camps and demonstrated again and again their loyalty as Americans.

These are but two of the many stories from history that can be found in the pages of the Lucent Books World History series. All World History titles rely on sound research and verifiable evidence, and all give students a clear sense of time, place, and chronology through maps and timelines as well as text.

All titles include a wide range of authoritative perspectives that demonstrate the complexity of historical interpretation and sharpen the reader's critical thinking skills. Formally documented quotations and annotated bibliographies enable students to locate and evaluate sources, often instantaneously via the Internet, and serve as valuable tools for further research and debate.

Finally, Lucent's World History titles present rousing good stories, featuring vivid primary source quotations drawn from unique, sometimes obscure sources such as diaries, public records, and contemporary chronicles. In this way, the voices of participants and witnesses as well as important biographers and historians bring the study of history to life. As we are caught up in the lives of others, we are reminded that we too are characters in the ongoing human saga, and we are better prepared for our own roles.

Important Dates in

2600s B.C.
The building of the Great Pyramid at Giza begins.

Ca. 563 B.C.
Siddhartha Gautama, founder of Buddhism, is born.

476
The Roman Empire collapses.

Ca. 570
The prophet Muhammad, founder of Islam, is born in Mecca.

1564
The great English playwright William Shakespeare is born.

1776
England's colonies in North America declare their independence, creating the United States.

B.C. 2600 — A.D. 200 — 500 — 800 — 1100 — 1400 — 1700 — 1800

Ca. 500 B.C.
Hinduism becomes a major religion in India.

Ca. A.D. 250
Mayan culture begins to flourish in Mesoamerica.

1204
Crusaders sack Constantinople, once the hub of the Byzantine world.

1492
Christopher Columbus reaches the West Indies, initiating a great age of global exploration.

1609
Italian astronomer Galileo builds a telescope and discovers mountains and craters on the moon.

1517
The Reformation, in which several Protestant sects break away from Roman Catholicism, begins.

10 ■ Religion and World Conflict

Religious World Conflict

1868
Japan begins a massive and momentous modernization program that will make it a world power.

1966
Mao Zedong launches the Cultural Revolution in China.

1997
Harry Potter and the Sorcerer's Stone, the first book in J.K. Rowling's hugely popular series, is published.

2006
An international organization of astronomers strips Pluto of its status as a planet.

1850　1900　　1950　2000

1929
The U.S. Stock Market crashes, launching a worldwide depression.

1947
Jackie Robinson breaks the color barrier in professiona baseball.

2001
Terrorists hijack commericial airliners and crash them into the World Trade Center, the Pentagon, and a Pennsylvania field.

1948
The modern State of Israel is established.

Important Dates in Religious World Conflict　11

Introduction

Killing in God's Name

During the morning of September 11, 2001, hundreds of millions of people gathered at television sets across the United States and around the world witnessed an unprecedented catastrophe. The vast majority were horrified and stunned by images of two hijacked airliners crashing with explosive impact into the World Trade Center towers in New York City. These structures, then among the tallest in the world, burst into flame. Within two hours, as hundreds of valiant firefighters attempted to rescue people trapped on the upper floors, both towers suddenly collapsed into gigantic piles of rubble and choking dust. Meanwhile, a third hijacked plane struck the Pentagon in Washington, D.C., and a fourth crashed in rural Pennsylvania. In all, some three thousand people died in these tragic attacks. This event and subsequent American efforts to find and punish those responsible marked the opening salvos of a conflict that many in the West call the "war on terrorism."

Perhaps even more tragic for many people was a disturbing revelation that emerged in the days following the September 11 disaster. U.S., British, and other international investigators found that these mass murders had been committed in the name of religion. Nineteen young Muslim men from Saudi Arabia and other Middle Eastern nations had perpetrated the crimes as part of a carefully crafted plan conceived by the leaders of the Islamic terrorist group known as al Qaeda, variously translated as "the Base" or "the Foundation." And they had done so while invoking the blessings and calling on the name of Allah, the god of Islam. A long letter later found in the belongings of one of the hijackers stated in part:

Do not seem confused or show signs of nervous tension. Be happy, optimistic, calm, because you are heading for a deed that God loves and will accept. . . . Remember that this is a battle for the sake of God. . . . When the confrontation begins . . . shout "God is great!" because this strikes fear into the hearts of the nonbelievers.[1]

Awakening from a Collective Amnesia

In the wake of the September 11 tragedy, a great many Americans and other Westerners were appalled, perplexed, and disheartened by reports that such a terrible act had been perpetrated in God's name. After all, most people living in Western countries belong to organized religions, including Christianity, Judaism, Islam, and others. And the vast majority of believers think that taking a human life is against God's wishes. Yet historians and others familiar with the long saga of humanity were quick to point out that killing in the name of religion is nothing new. Some suggested that people in today's progressive, industrialized countries—including the United States and most European nations

A ball of fire engulfs the hijacked airliner as it strikes the World Trade Center's remaining tower on September 11, 2001.

On September 11, 2001, horrified onlookers watch as the second tower of the World Trade Center disintegrates into a cloud of dust.

—had long suffered from a kind of collective historical amnesia. That is, they had forgotten that wars, battles, and assassinations committed in the name of God have occurred repeatedly in all corners of the globe throughout recorded history. As one of these scholars, James A. Haught, puts it:

> Time after time, in widely varied ways, faith spurs some believers to commit barbarism. The problem is a monster with a thousand faces. Millions of people think religion makes believers kind and brotherly, but there's an opposite side, a deeply disturbing one. Why does religion and its cultural ramifications impel some people to kill? No satisfactory answer has ever been found to this enigma.[2]

Nobel Prize–winning physicist Steven Weinberg echoes the same thought, adding that religiously motivated killing often occurs *within* a given faith as well as *between* rival faiths:

> Certainly good causes have sometimes been mobilized under the banner of religion, but . . . it's more often been the motivation for us to kill each other, not only for people of one religion to kill those of another, but even within religions.

After all, it was a Muslim who killed [Egyptian president Anwar] Sadat [in 1981]. It was a devout Jew who killed [Israeli prime minister Yitzhak] Rabin [in 1995]. It was a devout Hindu who killed [Indian nationalist and pacifist spiritual leader Mohandas] Gandhi [in 1948]. And this has been going on for centuries and centuries.[3]

Whether perpetrated within a faith or between faiths, so many murders have been committed and full-scale wars waged on account of religion it would be difficult to list them all. Among the more infamous of these holy horrors, as Haught calls them, were the Crusades; in this series of medieval wars, Christians and Muslims slaughtered one another for possession of the sacred city of Jerusalem and the holy lands surrounding it. Christians have murdered Jews throughout medieval and modern times; Christians have battled Christians in France, England, and other European countries in these same centuries; Hindus and Muslims have massacred each other in India; Protestants and Catholics have fought bitterly in Northern Ireland; and religious conflict has erupted in many more places and in many other eras.

Common Characteristics of Holy Wars

While the specific circumstances of these conflicts and massacres varied, nearly all of them had certain basic traits and characteristics in common. First, each involved some clearly defined religious goal. In the case of the September 11 attacks, for instance, al Qaeda's main goal was to force the United States and other Western countries to remove their troops and military bases from Islamic lands considered sacred soil in Saudi Arabia and other parts of the Middle East. Sometimes the main religious goal has been intertwined with political or economic motivations. Again in the case of al Qaeda, its leaders hoped (and still hope) to use violent means to weaken the economies of Western nations and expose their democratic systems as corrupt.

Second, nearly all holy wars and religiously motivated killings are led and sanctioned by a central, militant, and usually charismatic religious figure.

Killing in God's Name ■ 15

Al Qaeda's chief leader and ideologue is the Muslim fundamentalist Osama bin Laden, the son of a wealthy Saudi family. Most of his public statements have claimed in one way or another that al Qaeda's violent acts are the will of Allah. And many Muslims around the world think that Bin Laden was chosen by God to humble the West. Similarly, another infamous religious leader, seventeenth-century English soldier and politician Oliver Cromwell, believed he was chosen by God. Under God's banners, Cromwell, a staunch Puritan (a conservative Protestant sect), made himself England's dictator and persecuted Catholics.

A third characteristic common in religious wars, crusades, and killings has been the promise of some sort of rewards or salvation for those who take part. During the Crusades, for example, bishops and other church leaders promised Christian soldiers that they would ensure their own entrance into heaven by massacring Jewish and Muslim men, women, and children. And the nineteen hijackers who went to their deaths on September 11 did so believing that Allah would reward them in paradise.

Justification for Killing

In addition to promising their followers salvation and other rewards, leaders of religious wars have used various justifications to motivate the faithful. One common justification has been that resorting to violence can help spread the faith. Another justification—which became the main Christian rationale for the Crusades—was that going to war would free a holy site that had been captured by nonbelievers, or infidels. Still another way that holy wars and killings have been justified is when one religious group attacks another to avenge past acts of violence or blasphemy.

However, the most common and powerful justification for religiously motivated violence has been the notion that God wants and approves of the killing. To prove that this is so, the leaders of holy warriors typically fall back on the most militant or vengeful passages from sacred writings. Sections of the Koran, Islam's most holy book, for instance, have been invoked to justify jihad, an Arabic word often translated as "holy war." One passage of the Koran says:

> Allah will bring to nothing the deeds of those who disbelieve [in him] and debar others from his path.... The unbelievers follow falsehood, while the faithful follow truth from their Lord.... When you meet the unbelievers on the battlefield, strike off their heads and, when you have laid them low, bind your captives firmly.... Believers, if you help Allah, Allah will help you and make you strong. But the unbelievers shall be consigned to perdition. He will bring their deeds to nothing.[4]

Islam is not the only faith whose scriptures have been cited as justifications for war and murder. Through the

Believing his cause to be just, a crusading knight prays for strength in the holy wars he fights in the name of God.

Killing in God's Name ■ 17

centuries numerous Christian zealots have fallen back on passages from the Bible to defend or rationalize their violent acts. Often cited in this regard are the following verses from the Book of Deuteronomy:

> When you draw near to a city to fight against it, offer terms of peace to it.... If it makes no peace with you ... then you shall besiege it, and when the Lord your God gives it into your hand, you shall put all its males to the sword; but the women and the little ones, the cattle and everything else in the city, all its spoil you shall take as booty for yourselves, and you shall enjoy the spoil of your enemies, which the Lord your God has given you.[5]

To be sure, the Koran, Bible, and other widely venerated religious writings contain numerous passages that advocate positive paths, such as peace, brotherhood, and forgiveness. Yet over the course of many centuries, millions of people have chosen instead to embrace harsher divine directives like those above. Inspired by them, they have committed violent acts or made war in the name of a god or gods. It is impossible to know whether people would have acted on violent impulses *without* religious motivation. Religious fervor did and does play a role in world conflict, however, and has thus been the cause of much misery. This is the tragic side of religions that otherwise have produced much that is good and constructive. Perhaps no one has captured this sad side of the human story better than Weinberg. "With or without religion," he says, "good people can behave well and bad people can do evil; but for good people to do evil—that takes religion."[6]

Chapter One

Warfare Driven by Fundamentalist Beliefs

July 1, 1766, was a dark day in the French town of Abbeville. On that day a nineteen-year-old nobleman named Jean-François, Chevalier de la Barre was brutally executed at the insistence of local Catholic clergymen who claimed that the youth had defaced a crucifix on a bridge at the edge of town. Their only evidence was the denunciation of a local woman, who claimed de la Barre had sung a song that mocked the Christian faith and kept his hat on when a religious procession passed by. Surely, she said, the fact that he had committed such antireligious offenses proved he was the one who had harmed the crucifix. The priests agreed: Under torture the youth confessed and was sentenced to be beheaded and then burned at the stake. But when the influential French philosopher Voltaire heard about the case, he protested loudly. So higher authorities in France's legislature stepped in and offered to reduce de la Barre's sentence. Unlike Voltaire, however, they were afraid of what powerful church leaders would do to *them* if they were too lenient. So at their order the harsh sentence was carried out, and de la Barre became a symbol of religious persecution in France.

The gruesome death of Chevalier de la Barre was but a single case of killing driven by religious fundamentalism. In general, fundamentalists are members of a faith who strictly adhere to a set of basic, usually very old and conservative beliefs and who charge that those who do not accept these beliefs are misguided. The French priests who condemned de la Barre believed that ancient local Christian customs, such as removing one's hat during a religious procession, must be followed without exception. In their view, the slightest deviation from traditional beliefs and practices might weaken the faith throughout the

Warfare Driven by Fundamentalist Beliefs ■ 19

A painting depicts the pope being carried on his throne during a formal religious procession in the early 1600s.

community, which would surely bring down God's wrath on society as a whole. Like many fundamentalists, they opposed religious diversity and desired to see all people convert and conform to their personal religious views.

Fundamentalism has existed in every religion and in every age. Many fundamentalists would never go to the extremes of murder and mutilation—or even consider such actions. But some have been driven to violence when they were convinced that a core tenet of their faith had been violated. In 1980 in Moradabad, India, for example, Hindus and Muslims attacked one another after a pig walked across a patch of Muslim holy ground. The Muslims, who believe according to religious law that pigs are unclean, accused the Hindus of purposely unleashing the pig. Some two hundred people were killed in the riot that ensued.

The Sepoy Mutiny

Those involved in the pig riot reacted to what they saw as grave insults to their faith. A similar reaction occurred in the 1850s, when Indian soldiers called sepoys rebelled against the British, who then ruled India. The sepoys claimed the European occupiers had violated strict, sacred local religious laws.

The sepoys were Hindus, Muslims, and Sikhs who were trained by the occupying British to fight for British interests. As long as the British respected local customs, the sepoys remained loyal. But in 1857 the relationship between these native-born soldiers and their foreign-born commanders disintegrated. This change occurred when the British introduced a new rifle into India—the Enfield P/53. The sepoys viewed these guns as offensive and sacrilegious. Rutgers University scholar Bonnie G. Smith explains why:

> Soldiers had to bite the end off cartridges that had been greased with a mixture of beef and pork fat. The sepoys rebelled because beef and pork were meats forbidden to Hindus and Muslims respectively. . . . This blatant disregard for both sets of religious laws infuriated Indian soldiers.[7]

When some sepoys complained about the contaminated cartridges, army spokesmen promised that the rounds would be replaced with versions without beef or pork fat. But many sepoys suspected this was a lie designed to placate them. They felt defiled by British insensitivity to strict religious beliefs and customs. The commander in chief of British forces in India, George Anson, inflamed the situation further by callously saying: "I'll never give in to their beastly prejudices."[8] On May 9, 1857, eighty-five sepoy troopers stationed at Meerut,

Sepoys Turn on Their Officers

Many of the surviving eyewitness accounts of the Sepoy Mutiny are in the form of letters penned by British nationals residing in India. The following example was written by a British officer named Eckford to his brother-in-law in 1857, just as the rebellion was beginning.

About six o'clock on Sunday afternoon, the 10th of May last, I heard a great uproar in the direction of the Native Infantry and cavalry lines. It increased and I heard shots fired. On enquiring from my servants . . . they said the Native Troops [the sepoys] had mutinied and were setting fire to their lines and Officers' houses. I sent a man to find out and he said the sepoys were murdering their Officers.

Quoted in "India During the Raj: Eyewitness Accounts," Adams Matthew Publications. http://ampltd.tcuk.com/digital_guides/india_during_the_raj_parts_1_and_2/Publishers-Note-Part-2.aspx.

Warfare Driven by Fundamentalist Beliefs

In India, leaders of the Sepoy Mutiny are tied to guns by British troops in preparation for execution in 1857.

in northern India, refused to use the cartridges. As a result, they were publicly stripped of their uniforms and thrown in prison. Outraged sepoys stormed the stockade and released the prisoners, then went on a rampage and murdered every European they could find.

Within a week the mutiny had spread through large sections of northern and central India. Spurred by religious fervor, some of the rebellious sepoys conducted terrible mass killings. At Kanpur, for instance, as James Haught tells it,

> besieged and starving British troops surrendered on a promise that they and their wives and children would be allowed to leave safely. They were escorted as far as the Ganges River, then massacred. Some female survivors were kept several days, then executed with knives.[9]

In many cases British troops responded to such massacres by committing their own pitiless mass murders of prisoners.

But the mutiny was ultimately doomed. Fortunately for the British, not all the sepoys rebelled. For various reasons, the Sikhs, along with the Gurkhas in the far north, remained loyal to the British and helped defeat the Hindus and Muslims who had revolted. By June 1858 the rebellion was over. The punishments meted out by the British to captured rebels and their sympathizers were swift and brutal. Many sepoy prisoners were lashed to the fronts of cannons and blown to pieces when the weapons were fired. Entire villages of supposed rebel sympathizers were destroyed.

The Great Muslim Jihad

Religious fundamentalism also lay at the heart of the great Islamic jihad of the seventh and eighth centuries. Islam originated in Arabia in the early 600s when the prophet Muhammad began attracting followers in Medina, a city situated a few miles north of Mecca. Muhammad said that he had had an encounter with the angel Gabriel, who transmitted to Muhammad the word of Allah, which became the basis for Islam's holiest book, the Koran. Over the next few years, the new faith, based on the teachings of the Koran, spread to Mecca and other parts of Arabia.

Muhammad died in 632 but Islam survived and grew. The Prophet's most zealous followers decided that the best way to spread the faith was to launch military conquests into neighboring lands. In 634 the new caliph (meaning "successor" to Muhammad), Umar (or Omar) I, whipped his Arab troops into a state of religious and patriotic fervor. Syria fell to these troops in 636, Mesopotamia (now Iraq) between 637 and 641, Egypt in 642, and Iran in 651. Arab armies next surged across North Africa, and entered Spain, where they established an Islamic state in 711.

During these conquests, the invaders killed most of those who openly opposed them. However, large portions of

The Origins of Islam

Islam, one of the world's major religions, originated in Arabia in the early 600s. Shortly before, in about 571, a boy called al-Amin ("the Faithful") was born into the Quraysh tribe. Because his parents died when he was young, the boy was raised by his grandfather and a slave woman. As a young man, al-Amin became a merchant, but soon grew dissatisfied with his life. And not long afterward, according to tradition, he received a miraculous vision of the angel Gabriel. The latter's words to the young man became the basis of the Koran (the Muslim holy book) and the new faith of Islam. After being persecuted in Mecca (in western Arabia), al-Amin traveled to Jerusalem and then to Medina (north of Mecca), where he adopted the name Muhammad and gained many converts. Islam soon spread to Mecca and other parts of Arabia.

native populations were spared. Also, contrary to some popular accounts, the Muslim conquerors did not force all the defeated peoples to convert to Islam. As Bernard Lewis, a noted expert on Arab history, explains, the non-Muslim subjects of these lands

> were second-class citizens, paying a higher rate of taxation, suffering from certain social disabilities, and on a few rare occasions subjected to open persecution. But by and large . . . they enjoyed the free exercise of their religion, normal property rights, and were very frequently employed in the service of the state.[10]

Nevertheless, these peoples no longer controlled their own destiny. Moreover, as time went on most of them ended up converting to the faith of their conquerors—Islam. Some did so because it had become the dominant religion. Others converted so that they would be able to reap the economic benefits enjoyed by Muslims.

Indeed, strict adherence to Islam and its fundamental principles and ideas contributed to the phenomenal success of the Muslim Arab conquests, as well as to the longevity of the Islamic empire. Unquestioning belief in Allah and rigid observance of the principles laid down in the Koran helped bolster the determination and courage of Arab tribesmen who were often ill-equipped and outnumbered by their enemies. It also established the Koran's authority as the source of all truth and wisdom,

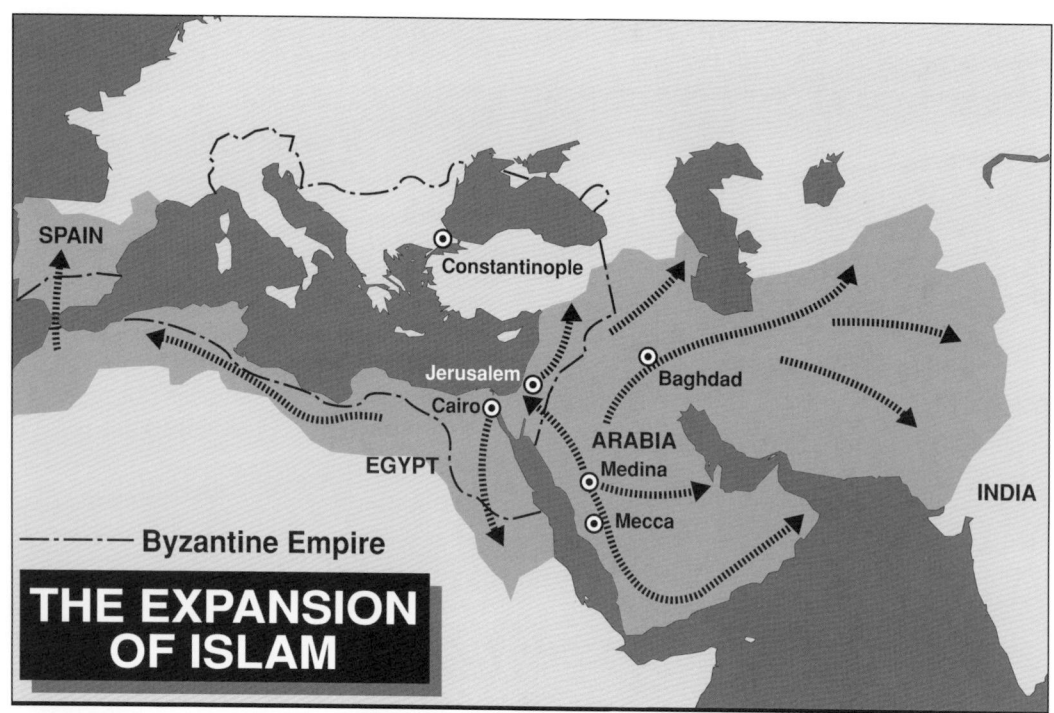

24 ■ Religion and World Conflict

which minimized the influence of (and possible competition from) rival sects. "Surely the major determinant of Arab success," writes historian William H. McNeill,

> was the discipline and courage inspired in the rank and file by the certainty, confirmed with each victory, that Allah was indeed fighting on their side.... The effort to remake human life according to the will of Allah ... was equally significant in the cultural sphere. In its most extreme form, radical piety entailed suspicion of any activity not directly serving the ends of religion. Truth and beauty resided in the Koran. Any other repository [of knowledge and law], being merely human, distracted people from the pursuit of holiness.... Thus, the scope of orthodox Muslim culture remained remarkably narrow.[11]

The Muslim Assault on Europe

Elements of this narrow fundamentalist outlook remain alive and well among some factions of Islam today, especially those that try to achieve their goals by advocating and committing violence. Certainly the militant Muslims of the early eighth century believed that it was their duty to bring all known lands into the Islamic empire. To this end, after overrunning Spain the Arab armies regrouped and began to move northward into what is now France. The long-term goal was to bring all of Europe under Arab rule and, hopefully, over time to convert the Europeans to Islam. If this goal had been achieved, much of the succeeding history of the world would have been radically different.

At first, the Arab invaders, commanded by the governor of Muslim Spain, 'Abd ar-Rahnan al Ghafiqi, enjoyed some successes. He and his troops penetrated deeply into France and raided the town of Autun, about 200 miles [322km] southeast of Paris, in 725. In the following year, Carcassonne (in southern France) and Nîmes (in southeastern France, near the Mediterranean coast) fell to the Arabs. At the time, the Franks, former Germanic tribesmen who had settled in France during the preceding two centuries, were divided into rival factions with separate leaders. This lack of unity weakened the Franks militarily and gave the invaders an important advantage. It appeared that the Arabs might overrun the region and then move on into Germany and other neighboring lands.

Then, around 732, one of the Frankish chieftains, Charles Martel, gathered as many Frankish soldiers as possible in hopes of halting the Arab advance. Martel also managed to convince troops from another strong Germanic tribe, the Burgundians, to join his cause. By this time, 'Abd ar-Rahnan had reached Poitiers (in west-central France) and was moving northward toward Tours. Hearing that the Franks were speeding toward him, he led his own troops

The Frankish chieftain Charles Martel (shown on horseback) proclaims victory over the Muslims at the critical Battle of Tours in 732.

eastward. Somewhere to the east of Poitiers and Tours (the exact location remains unknown), the two armies met in what turned out to be one of the most decisive battles in history.

The exact manner in which the Arabs and Franks fought the Battle of Tours is uncertain. Some evidence suggests that Martel arranged his foot soldiers, or infantry, in a huge square and that the Arabs were unable to penetrate the formation. A surviving Arab chronicle provides more information and describes the fate of 'Abd ar-Rahnan:

26 ■ Religion and World Conflict

Near the river Owar [the Loire], the two great hosts of the two languages and the two creeds [Christianity and Islam] were set in array against each other.... The Muslim horsemen dashed fiercely and frequently forward against the battalions of the Franks, who resisted manfully, and many fell dead on either side, until the going-down of the sun.... Many of the Muslims were fearful for the safety of the spoil [booty taken from captured towns] which they had stored in their tents... and several squadrons of the Muslim horsemen rode off to protect their tents. ... And while 'Abd ar-Rahnan strove to [stop them] and lead them back to battle, the warriors of the Franks came round him and he was pierced through with many spears, so that he died. Then all the [Arab] host fled before the enemy, and many died in the flight.[12]

With their leader dead and the battle lost, the Arabs retreated southward toward their Spanish kingdom. Martel and his men had saved their own country, and likely much if not all of the rest of Europe, from Muslim domination. However, the Arabs continued their raids into southern France for some time to come. And they remained a potential threat to Europe for many more centuries. Not until 1492 did the Spanish Christian monarchs Ferdinand and Isabella (who also supplied explorer Christopher Columbus with ships for his voyage across the Atlantic) achieve the surrender of Granada, the last Muslim stronghold in Spain.

Fighting the Forces of Satan

During the 1400s, with the Arab threat fast receding, Europeans began to encounter another onslaught of violence motivated by fundamentalist beliefs. This time the culprits were Christians. In fact, they were priests and other officials of the Western Church, led by the pope in Rome, who conducted a series of witch hunts that lasted for some three centuries. During this period the church, seeing itself literally at war with the forces of Satan, killed at least several hundred thousand innocent people. (Some scholars place the death toll as high as 2 million.)

Europe's great series of witch hunts originally grew out of the formation and expansion of the Holy Inquisition. This commission or organization within the church was created in the 1230s with the goal of stamping out heresy, any perceived opposition to or lack of adherence to the established religious order and its most basic beliefs. The popes sent out inquisitors, in a sense special prosecutors, to root out, bring to trial, condemn, and if necessary execute the supposed enemies of the faith. The inquisitors came from many different ranks of the priesthood, but a large proportion of them were Dominican monks.

Among the heretics the inquisitors looked for were witches. In medieval times witches were usually perceived as women, but also sometimes men, who were in league with Satan and his dark forces. Typical accusations against witches were that they engaged in sexual acts with Satan or his demons, transformed themselves into animals, flew through the sky, made themselves invisible, or tried to corrupt ordinary God-fearing folk. Although a few accused witches were executed in the 1200s and 1300s, the witch hunts became large-scale only after Pope Innocent VIII issued an edict in 1484. This document declared not only that witches were real but that anyone who did not believe in witches was also a heretic who must be punished. In 1486 two Dominican inquisitors published the *Malleus Maleficarum*, or *Witches' Hammer*. This infamous guidebook listed the supernatural acts

A French engraving details the horrific punishment of a woman accused of being a witch as other accused women await execution.

This painting by Francisco de Goya depicts a tribunal judging suspected heretics during the Holy Inquisition by the Christian church.

28 ■ Religion and World Conflict

performed by witches and told how witches caused disease, destroyed crops, and kidnapped and ate children.

Sanctioned by the popes and their bishops, the Inquisition conducted witch hunts in Germany, France, Italy, Spain, Sweden, Switzerland, and elsewhere in Europe. These persecutions eventually reached England and led to the famous 1692 trials of witches in Salem, in New England's Massachusetts Bay Colony. Most of the supposed witches were women whose names had been shouted out by other women being tortured by inquisitors. Indeed, after their arrest, suspected witches were usually subjected to gruesome tortures to force confessions of witchcraft and to reveal the names of new suspects. "The victims were stripped naked [and] shaved of all body hair," Haught writes: "Fingernails were pulled out. Red-hot tongs were applied to breasts. . . . Bodies were stretched on racks and wheels. Virtually every mangled and broken victim confessed—and was executed on the basis of the confession."[13]

The hysteria over witchcraft gradually subsided and by 1700 the number of witches accused and arrested in Europe had decreased dramatically. Yet a few women were still victimized after that, even as the rise of modern science raised major doubts about the authenticity of witchcraft. The last legalized execution of a witch occurred in 1782 in Switzerland. But the centuries of persecution and carnage based on fundamentalist intolerance and paranoia still remains a blot on the church's reputation and a shameful chapter in the history of the faith.

Cromwell and the Puritans

Some Europeans who felt that the church had gone too far in its brutal witch hunts came to see another series of fundamentalist abuses as divine or poetic justice. This was because a great many of the victims in the new round of persecutions, which took place in England and Ireland, were followers of the church of Rome, or Catholics. The groundwork for these anti-Catholic crusades was laid during the Protestant Reformation of the 1500s, when England's King Henry VIII separated his country from the authority of the popes. Angered by the pope's refusal to grant him a divorce, Henry established the Church of England, a Protestant denomination of Christianity also known as the Anglican Church, with himself as its supreme head. Under the new religious order, Catholics, especially wealthy and powerful ones, became increasingly unpopular.

But even as anti-Catholic sentiment grew in England, some devoutly religious Englishmen came to see both the new Church of England and the papacy as corrupt and tyrannical. Because these Protestant fundamentalists wanted to purify the church and reassert the primacy of the Bible over worldly authority, the sect they formed became known as Puritans. Not surprisingly, both Anglican and Roman Catholic leaders, including the reigning monarchs, resented the Puritans' interference and the result was

The Puritans Capture Drogheda

Oliver Cromwell recorded his own account of the storming of the Irish city of Drogheda in 1649. After he and his Puritan troops took the city, they massacred more than three thousand of the survivors.

Although our men that stormed the breeches [barricades] were forced to recoil [pull back] . . . being encouraged to recover their loss, they made a second attempt, wherein God was pleased to animate them [and] they [gained] ground of the enemy, and by the grace of God forced him to quit his entrenchments. And after a very hot dispute [fight], the enemy . . . gave ground, and our men became masters of [most of the town]. . . . Being in the heat of action, I forbade [my soldiers] to spare any that were in arms in the town, and, I think, that night they put to the sword about 2,000 men.

Quoted in Wilbur C. Abbot, ed., *The Writings and Speeches of Oliver Cromwell*, vol. 2. Cambridge, MA: Harvard University, 1939, pp. 126–27.

Oliver Cromwell leads his Puritan followers through the streets of Drogheda in 1649.

Warfare Driven by Fundamentalist Beliefs

King Charles I of England is led to his execution in 1649.

a series of persecutions of the Puritans in the early 1600s. Fleeing these persecutions, some Puritans moved to Holland; others crossed the Atlantic and established a North American colony at Plymouth, in what is now the commonwealth of Massachusetts.

But the Puritans persevered and eventually, if briefly, they triumphed. Over the years they gained many sympathizers in Parliament, England's primary legislative body. Then, in the early 1640s King Charles I had a serious falling-out with Parliament after he attempted to arrest its leaders, along with several Puritans. The king's enemies proceeded to form a rival government and raise troops. A bloody, four-year-long civil war ensued, during which Oliver Cromwell, a Puritan who had earlier served in Parliament, took charge of the forces opposing the king.

Cromwell and his Puritan followers turned their army into a religious as well as military organization. The soldiers, who became known as "Ironsides," carried Bibles with them everywhere and sang hymns while marching. All battles were preceded by mass recitals of prayers and any victories were attributed to God, whom the Puritans claimed was on their side. As Cromwell himself stated:

> A great thing should be done, not by power or might, but by the Spirit of God. And is it not so clear? That which caused your men to storm [into battle] so courageously, it was the Spirit of God, who gave your men courage and . . . therewith this happy success. And therefore it is good that God alone have all the glory.[14]

King Charles lost the civil war and Parliament set limits on his power. But he was reluctant to stay within these limits and Cromwell eventually led the radical movement to try Charles for treason and sentence him to death. Charles was executed in 1649, by which time Cromwell, with the army under his complete control, had become virtual dictator.

In the years that followed, the remaining Catholics in England and Ireland suffered under the rule of the Puritans, who hated the pope and viewed Catholics as vermin. Led by Cromwell, who now bore the title of Lord Protector, the Puritans crossed into Ireland and began slaughtering Catholics and Protestants who sympathized with the Catholics. After much hard fighting, the city of Drogheda surrendered. Cromwell's troops then sacked the city and massacred some 3,550 prisoners, including women and priests. Cromwell called the violence "a righteous judgment of God upon these barbarous wretches,"[15] and went on to massacre another two thousand Catholics in the Irish town of Wexford.

In addition to committing mass murder, the Puritans attempted to remake English society, banning all forms of public entertainment, including dancing and going to the theater. They called such activities frivolous and against God's will. Because of these excesses, large numbers of Englishmen, including both Catholics and Protestants, came to loathe the Puritan regime. And after Cromwell died in 1658, there was an enormous backlash. In what came to be called the Restoration, the monarchy was restored and Puritans were hounded out of public posts. As has happened in all cases of violence, conquest, and murder inspired by fundamentalist ideology, more moderate and tolerant forces inevitably prevailed.

Chapter Two

Holy Wars for Territory and Political Power

The civil war and Puritan dictatorship that gripped England in the mid-1600s was driven in large degree by fundamentalist Christian beliefs. However, these violent disruptions were also about the desire to acquire and wield military and political power. The Puritans, led by the dictator Oliver Cromwell, imposed their will on the country and tried to gain territory and political power in Ireland as well.

It is not unusual for religious causes to mask political motives. Religious faith and devotion have been used as excuses or pretexts for gaining power and land throughout history. The ancient Assyrian kings, for example, who forged a great empire in what is now Iraq in the early first millennium B.C., justified their conquests partly on religious grounds. The wars they waged and the harsh rule they imposed on others was, they said, guided and sanctified by their chief god, the mighty Ashur. Later, in Italy in A.D. 312, Constantine, a leading claimant to Rome's imperial throne, justified his own bid for power by calling on divine forces. Constantine wanted to oust another royal claimant, Maxentius, who had seized the venerable city of Rome. Among Constantine's closer followers were members of the Christian sect, who before this time had suffered horrible persecutions under the Romans. Constantine had his soldiers paint Christian symbols on their shields in hopes that the Christian god would help him achieve victory and ultimate power. This plan worked, or at least Constantine believed it did. In a desperate battle fought at Rome's Milvian Bridge, he decisively defeated Maxentius and afterward marched into Rome in triumph.

The Middle Ages, the roughly thousand-year period in Europe following Rome's fall, witnessed some of

Protestants and Catholics battle in 1632 at Lützen, Germany, during the bloody Thirty Years War.

the largest and bloodiest holy wars ever fought for territory or power. The Crusades, a series of conflicts waged from 1095 to 1291, pitted Christian invaders against Muslims for control of the Holy Land. And in the 1600s, at the same time that the Puritans were rising to power in England, continental Europe was torn asunder by the Thirty Years War. This truly disastrous conflict fought between Catholics and Protestants left at least 3 million (and possibly as many as 8 million) people dead and transformed large portions of Europe into rubble-strewn wastelands.

Modern history has also been plagued by religiously motivated struggles for territory or power. Perhaps the most familiar of these struggles erupted in the first half of the twentieth century between Arabs and Jews in Palestine. Each side believed, and still believes, that God granted it rightful possession of the lands making up the modern nation of Israel. Similar violence, this time between Christians and Muslims, erupted in the 1950s in Sudan, in North Africa. In a struggle that continued until 2005, the Muslims, who hold political and military power in the country, wanted to keep Christians and other non-Muslims powerless and even to eradicate them.

"God Wills It"

The hatred and rivalry between Christians and Muslims in modern Sudan in a way echoed the many violent episodes that occurred during the medieval Crusades. One major difference is that the strife in Sudan was instigated mainly by Muslims against Christians. The holy wars of the Crusades, in contrast, were primarily instigated by Christians against Muslims. These conflicts started in 1095 at the urgings of Pope Urban II, leader of the Western Christian Church centered in Rome. Urban knew that the holy city of Jerusalem had long been under Arabic Muslim rule. (The Muslims had captured the city in 638 during their great jihad.) The pope also knew that the Arab Muslims, who revered Jesus Christ as one of their prophets, had long allowed Christian pilgrims to visit Jerusalem unmolested. In 1071, however, a different Muslim group, the Seljuk Turks, had captured Jerusalem and began taxing and sometimes mistreating Christian pilgrims. Pope Urban felt that he had to do something to aid these pilgrims.

It was the manner in which the pope tried to help Christian pilgrims that caused most of the trouble. Instead of sending ambassadors to negotiate some kind of peaceful agreement, he called on the Christian nobles of Europe and their knights and armies to go to war to oust the Muslims from the Holy Land and bring that region under Christian control. Urban proclaimed:

> The Lord prays and exhorts [urges] you, as heralds of Christ to urge men of all ranks, knights and foot-soldiers, rich and poor, to hasten to exterminate this vile race from the [Holy Land], and to bear timely aid to the worshippers of Christ.... Oh, what a disgrace if a race so despised, degenerate, and slave of demons, should thus conquer a people fortified with faith in omnipotent [all-powerful] God and resplendent with the name of Christ![16]

Urban's call, which included the words *Deus Vult*, or "God wills it," launched the so-called First Crusade, which lasted from 1095 to 1099. Tens of thousands of people from all across Europe followed various leaders—some powerful noblemen, others mere rabble-rousers—in huge marches that moved eastward across Europe. Some gave their allegiance to a priest named Peter the Hermit, who claimed that Jesus himself had come to him and sanctioned the war. Other priests led their own detachments of crusaders, as did a number of dukes and other nobles recruited by the pope. In all, as many as seventy thousand fighting men had traveled to the Middle East by 1097. They were accompanied by thousands

The Pope Stirs Up Hatred for Muslims

As part of his effort to convince European Christians to launch a holy war to gain control of the Holy Land, Pope Urban II cited numerous atrocities supposedly committed by Muslims against Christians. It is likely that most of these incidents were either false or exaggerated. The pope stated in part:

From the confines of Jerusalem and the city of Constantinople [now Istanbul in Turkey] a horrible tale has gone forth . . . namely, that a race from the kingdom of the Persians . . . a race utterly alienated from God . . . has invaded the lands of those Christians and has depopulated them by the sword, pillage and fire; it has led away a part of the captives into its own country, and a part it has destroyed by cruel tortures; it has either entirely destroyed the churches of God or taken them over to use for the rites of their own religion. They destroy the altars, after having defiled them with their uncleanness. . . . When they wish to torture people by a base death, they perforate their navels, and dragging forth the . . . intestines, bind it to a stake; then with flogging they lead the victim around until, the insides having gushed forth, the victim falls prostrate upon the ground. . . . Let the holy sepulcher [sacred tomb] of the Lord our Savior, which is possessed by unclean nations, especially incite you, and the holy places which are now . . . irreverently polluted with their filthiness.

Quoted in Norton Downs, ed., *Basic Documents in Medieval History.* Melbourne, FL: Krieger, 1992, pp. 75–76.

To create support for the Crusades, Pope Urban II (pictured) encouraged the belief that Muslims were evil.

of squires, merchants, laborers, and other supporters.

Many people today find it remarkable that so many people of all walks of life left their families and jobs behind to fight and maybe to die in a strange, faraway place. But the Roman Church held extraordinary power over the hearts and minds of Europeans in the medieval era. The vast majority of the crusading knights and foot soldiers, as well as the civilians who followed them, were filled with genuine religious zeal. They believed that their faith was the only true faith and must be defended to the death. In their view, God had called on them to go to the Holy Land to fight and afterward to pray on the very ground where Jesus and his disciples had once walked.

Jerusalem Taken, Then Lost

Motivated by such religious fervor, the crusaders besieged Jerusalem in July 1099. One of the attackers, a Frenchman named Fulk of Chartres, later penned a description of the event, which reads in part:

> The [Christian] leaders ordered scaling ladders to be made, hoping that by a brave assault it might be possible to surmount [climb] the walls by means of the ladders and thus take the city. . . . It was [also] ordered that siege machines should be constructed. . . . When the [siege] tower had been put together and had been covered with hides, it was moved nearer to the wall. Then knights, few in number, but brave, at the sound of the trumpet took their places in the tower and began to shoot stones and arrows. [After many such assaults] on Friday [July 15, 1099], with trumpets sounding, [and] amid great commotion and shouting, "God help us," the Franks entered the city.[17]

After massacring thousands of people in Jerusalem, the Europeans took charge of the city and set up several small Christian states in the area. Collectively, these principalities came to be called the Outremer, or "lands overseas." But the Christians were unable to hold onto Jerusalem. It was recaptured by the Muslims in 1187, and it became clear that the Outremer was in danger of falling, too. Europeans responded by launching more crusades with the goal of retaking Jerusalem and protecting the crusader states in the area. Modern scholars still debate the total number of expeditions that can be called the full-scale Crusades, but most agree that there were at least seven or eight. Ultimately, however, these expeditions failed to maintain a permanent European foothold. By the late 1200s all of the states in the Outremer had fallen. In Haught's words, "Two centuries of death and destruction had been for nothing."[18]

Moreover, the thousands of soldiers from the opposing armies who were killed and the inhabitants of Jerusalem who were massacred were not the only casualties of these holy wars. It became

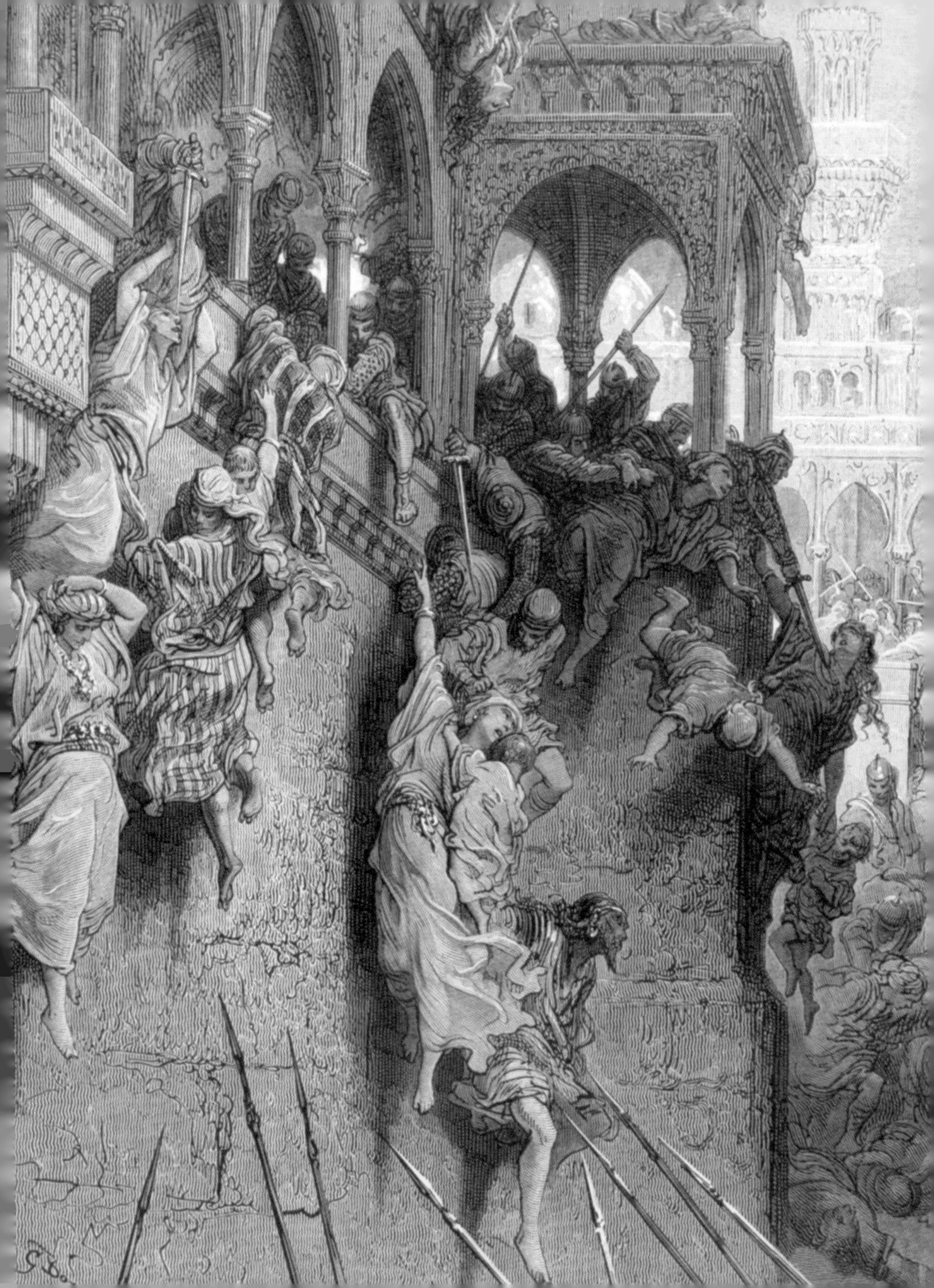

common practice, for instance, for crusaders on the march to slaughter Jews living in European cities situated on the way to the Holy Land. Tens of thousands of Jews—men, women, and children—suffered torture and rape and met hideous deaths. More than eight thousand Jews were killed in the German town of Worms alone. And any Christians who tried to save them were butchered as well.

Many later European historians, poets, and other writers attempted to cast these wars and massacres in a good light. Poems, novels, and eventually films all tended to depict the Crusades not only as necessary, but also as colorful, chivalrous adventures. But this distorted vision obscures the more terrible truth. "Through the haze of legend," Haught writes,

> the Crusades are remembered as a romantic quest by noble knights wearing crimson crosses. In reality, the Crusades were a sickening nightmare of slaughter, rape, looting, and chaos. . . . The crusaders killed nearly as many Christians and Jews as they did Muslims, their intended target.[19]

Large numbers of Muslims did die in the Crusades. And the survivors passed on their own, quite disparaging version

Innocent Muslim women and children are slain during a frenzied attack on Jerusalem by Christians during the Crusades.

of these wars to later generations. The common view in Islamic cities and states in succeeding centuries was that, as Oxford University scholar Christopher Tyerman puts it, "a civilized medieval Islamic world [was] brutalized by Western barbarians."[20] This attitude has periodically fueled anti-Western feeling among Muslims, including in recent times. Shortly before ordering the invasion of Iraq in 2003, for example, U.S. president George W. Bush remarked to the press about his ongoing "crusade" against terrorists. His intended meaning was a righteous campaign to capture and punish a band of criminals but Muslims around the world immediately interpreted the remark as an insensitive reference to a holy war against any and all who practice Islam.

The Horrors of the Thirty Years War

Among the more regrettable aspects of the Crusades were the numerous instances of vandalism, looting, and murder that took place in European cities as the crusader armies marched eastward. Sadly, many of these same cities suffered again from religiously motivated violence only a few centuries later.

From 1618 to 1648, large portions of Europe were ravaged by one of the most destructive wars ever fought in the world up to that time. Called the Thirty Years War, the conflict erupted primarily out of deep-seated religious differences between Catholic and Protestant factions in Germany. At the time, Germany was not a united country, as

An engraving depicts Protestant rebels hurling Roman Catholic officials through a palace window in Prague in 1618, an incident that sparked the Thirty Years War.

it is today, but was made up of several small, independent rival states that were committed to be either Catholic or Protestant by a 1555 treaty. Some of the rulers of these states formed the Protestant Union in 1608. A year later others created the Catholic League. Though these alliances were formed mainly for defensive purposes, both eventually went on the offensive after growing tensions between Catholics and Protestants reached the breaking point. When some Protestant noblemen tossed two Catholic priests out of a palace window in the city of Prague, an army raised by the Catholic League slaughtered a contingent of the Protestant Union.

As the great war commenced in 1618, the strongest of the German Catholic princes, Ferdinand II, further inflamed the situation by launching a large-scale religious persecution. It was designed to eliminate every Protestant from the German region and leave Catholics

42 ■ Religion and World Conflict

with all the land and political power. Not surprisingly, local Protestants responded by appealing for aid from the rulers of other European nations. And soon Denmark, Sweden, France, Spain, and other countries entered the fray. At first, the many armies, large and small, involved in the fighting attacked only enemy forces. But as time went on many of the soldiers became renegades and veritable pirates who raided both Catholic and Protestant villages at will, spreading destruction and misery far and wide. Typical was the sacking and wholesale destruction of the Protestant German town of Magdeburg, recalled in this eyewitness account:

Then was there naught but beating and burning, plundering, torture, and murder. Most especially was every one of the enemy bent on securing much booty.... The great and splendid city that had stood like a fair princess in the land was now ... given over to flames, and

In 1648 representatives from various countries review and sign the Treaty of Westphalia, which concluded the Thirty Years War.

Holy Wars for Territory and Political Power

thousands of innocent men, women, and children, in the midst of a horrible din of heart-rending shrieks and cries, were tortured and put to death in so cruel and shameful a manner that no words would suffice to describe [it].[21]

An estimated twenty thousand residents of Magdeburg were massacred, leaving about four hundred battered, terrorized souls squatting in the city's charred ruins. In addition to such wanton sacking of towns, the war caused the destruction of large tracts of farmland, orchards, and vineyards, resulting in famine in some areas. In addition, debilitating diseases, including typhus, dysentery, and bubonic plague, spread through Germany, Italy, and other areas, wiping out tens of thousands of people.

The Thirty Years War finally ended in 1648 with the signing of the Treaty of Westphalia. This war spawned by religious hatred and the desire for power ended up having momentous consequences for later generations of Europeans and Americans. First, Germany emerged from the war in a state of utter devastation and as disunited as ever. Local bitterness over the destruction wrought by outsiders later contributed to the growth of militant German nationalism, an important factor in World Wars I and II. Meanwhile, Spain, once one of Europe's strongest nations, lost much power and influence, while France emerged as the continent's dominant power.

Another far-reaching consequence of the war was the way it affected the development of political ideas in the century that followed. When the Founding Fathers of the infant United States drew up its Constitution in the late 1700s, the horrors of the Thirty Years War were still fresh in their minds. They instituted strict separation of church and state partly as a way of avoiding such destructive wars based on religious differences.

Killing Over Land in Israel

Thanks to the foresight of the American founders, the United States has indeed been spared wars based on religious rivalries and attempts by religious groups to acquire power and territory. Other parts of the world have not been as fortunate, however. One of the most bitter ongoing disputes of this kind is that between Arabs and Israelis. From 1948, when the modern State of Israel was established, to the present day, several bloody wars have been fought between Arabs and Jews. And the violence takes other forms as Palestinian Arab suicide bombers frequently attack Israeli towns and the Israeli military strikes out at Palestinians.

The differences between the two sides are based mainly on competing claims to the land and the right to settle on it. Both Arabs and Jews claim a historic

This painting presents a romanticized version of the death of General Charles George Gordon at the hands of the Mahdi in Khartoum in 1885.

Religion and World Conflict

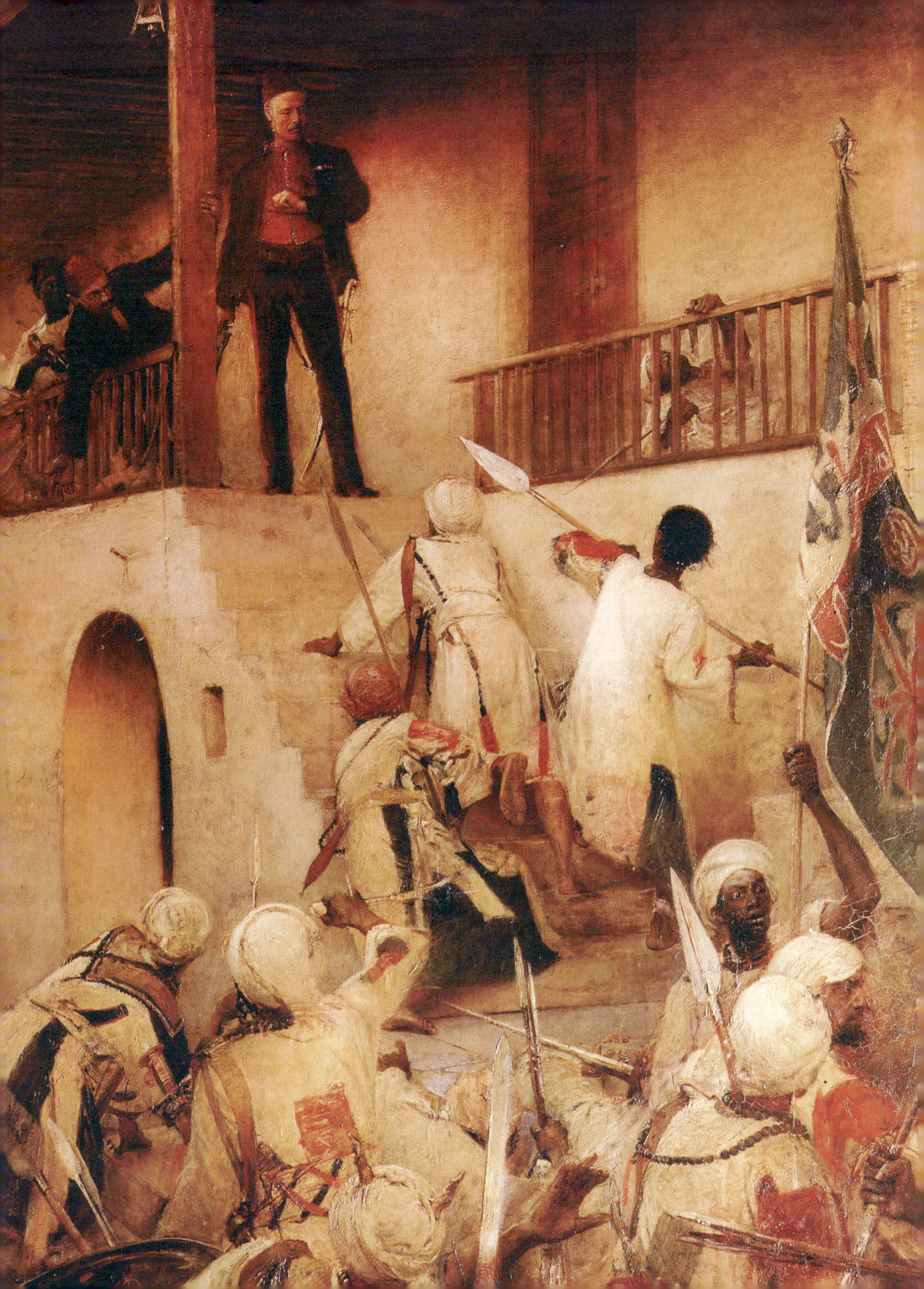

General Gordon Versus the Mahdi

One of the major incidents that fueled hatred between Muslims and Christians and eventually led to two civil wars in Sudan was the face-off between two larger-than-life figures at Khartoum in 1884–1885. Britain's General Charles George Gordon had served as governor of Sudan for the Egyptians in the 1870s. He was a fundamentalist Christian who saw himself as an agent of God, which proved ironic because his opponent at Khartoum, Muhammad Ahmad, a Sudanese Muslim, was an Islamic fundamentalist who claimed to be the Mahdi, or "enlightened one sent by God." The Mahdi decided that the Egyptians and British were corrupt and must be driven out of Sudan. And he defeated several Egyptian armies sent to stop him. In 1884 Gordon was asked to go to Khartoum and organize its evacuation, but he became trapped there when the Mahdi's forces attacked. On January 28, 1885, the city fell after a ten-month siege and Gordon was killed in the fighting.

connection to the land that is now Israel. And both groups cite the will of God to support their presence there. They have fought many wars and many on both sides have died as a result of ongoing hostilities.

Civil Wars in Sudan

Religiously motivated violence has also claimed the lives of thousands in Sudan. Africa's largest nation, Sudan is located south of Egypt and west of Ethiopia. The civil wars that wracked Sudan in the twentieth century grew out of religious, ethnic, and political troubles that began in the previous century. Egypt took control of the northern part of Sudan in 1820. But when the Egyptians attempted to extend their control farther south in the 1870s, they encountered resistance. They called on the noted British military general Charles George Gordon (1833–1885) to help organize the region. Gordon also served as governor of Sudan for the Egyptians. In 1885 Gordon was killed when a Muslim extremist named Muhammad Ahmed, known as the Mahdi, or "enlightened one," led a rebellion and captured the leading Sudanese city of Khartoum. The Egyptians then abandoned Sudan, where the Mahdi set up a strict fundamentalist Islamic state. That regime was short-lived, however, for the British and Egyptians invaded in the late 1890s and Sudan became in effect a British colony.

As long as the British ruled Sudan, tensions between the mostly Arab Muslim north and mostly black African Christian south remained under control. But in 1955 the British announced that they were planning to grant the region its independence the following year. Fearing oppression by the northern Muslims, some of the southern black tribes rebelled. And just as the British withdrew, a major civil war broke out. That bloody conflict raged until an agreement was signed in 1972, leaving half a million people dead and more than 750,000 homeless.

But the truce between the warring factions did not last long. In 1983 Sudanese president Gaafar Muhammad al-Nimeiry, a Muslim, imposed a series of harsh Islamic laws on the entire country, including the severing of hands and other body parts for theft and other minor infractions. Many people around the world, including some Muslims, protested that imposing these laws violated the human rights of the Sudanese Christians in the south, which had been granted considerable autonomy by the 1972 agreement. But al-Nimeiry and his followers refused to listen to reason. The result was another religiously motivated, prolonged, and deadly civil war. Some 250,000 southern Sudanese died in 1988 alone. And by 2005, when a treaty finally established a shaky peace, a total of 2.2 million southern Sudanese Christians had been killed. (That same year, a new rebellion erupted in Darfur, a province in western Sudan. The new conflict pits violent Arab militia groups against local black settlers in Darfur and is motivated more by racial and ethnic disputes than by religious differences.)

The civil wars in Sudan clearly show that the religious tensions that brought about the Crusades nearly a thousand years ago have not dissipated. Christians and Muslims still vie for land and power in various corners of the globe. And at times they are willing to fight and die over their differences.

Chapter Three

Religious Hatred and Revenge

Some of the worst wars, mass murders, and other outbreaks of violence in history have been motivated by religious hatred or revenge. And often the roots of such violence and hatred are found in an event or grievance that occurred hundreds or even thousands of years earlier.

This hate-revenge scenario is well illustrated by recurring violent episodes in India in modern times between Hindus, Muslims, and Sikhs. Often, distrust and hatred among these faiths festers for months or years and then suddenly surfaces in an explosion of vandalism and killing. In 1984, for example, a local Hindu leader in a town near Bombay delivered an anti-Muslim speech to his followers. This led to violent riots between Hindus and Muslims in which 216 people died, 756 were wounded, and some 13,000 had their homes seriously damaged or destroyed.

Christians, too, have been both perpetrators and targets of religious revenge killings. In A.D. 64, Christianity was still a new and small religious sect in the Roman Empire. The emperor Nero accused the Christians of igniting the great fire that destroyed large portions of the city of Rome that year. (He needed a scapegoat because many Romans suspected, probably mistakenly, that he himself had started the fire.) Hundreds of Christians were tied to large crosses or stakes, shot with arrows, and burned to death. These revenge killings were the first of many anti-Christian persecutions instituted by the Romans in the three centuries that followed. Ironically, in the late 300s, when the Christians finally prevailed and took over Rome's government, they turned the tables. It became common for crowds of Christian Romans to seek revenge on non-Christian Romans by vandalizing pagan temples.

And later, in medieval and modern times, many Christians perpetrated revenge killings against Jews. This was based in part on the twisted belief that all Jews, no matter when or where they were born, were responsible for the death of Jesus Christ.

In fact, no single religious group in history has been persecuted and targeted for death more than the Jews. Ever since the ancient Jewish kingdoms of Israel and Judah were destroyed by the Assyrians and Babylonians in the first millennium B.C., the Jews have suffered from hatred and discrimination. Almost always, anti-Semitism (hatred for and discrimination against Jews) has stemmed from ignorance or misconceptions about what Jews believe, how they worship, and what they did in history. Tragically, such all-but-unshakable misperceptions have led to mindless killing. The slaughter of Jews by Christian crusaders on their way to the Holy Land is only one of numerous examples.

Christ-Killers and Blood Libels

Indeed, hatred for Jews among Christians originated long before the Crusades. Although Jesus and his earliest

An artist depicts the court of emperor Nero, who ordered hundreds of Christians killed after falsely accusing them of starting the great fire of Rome.

Long persecuted for their beliefs, Jews are burned at the stake in France in this medieval manuscript illumination.

followers were all Jews, medieval Christians came to despise the Jews. Part of this enmity may have derived from an attempt by early Christians to distance themselves from a people widely viewed as fanatical and rebellious. A succession of foreign peoples, including Babylonians, Greeks, and Romans, occupied the Jewish homelands in what is now Israel in the late first millennium B.C. and early first millennium A.D. The Jews, constantly rebelling and attempting to reinstate their autonomy, were branded as troublemakers. For some Christians (after they split from Judaism in the mid-to-late first century), denouncing the Jews was one way of emphasizing that they themselves were no longer Jews.

The notion that the Jewish people had aided and abetted the Romans in crucifying Jesus Christ in Jerusalem in about A.D. 30 added to Christian animosity toward Jews. So, when Christians

Possessed by Demons?

Among the many texts that incited violence against Jews in the Middle Ages were the widely quoted anti-Semitic lectures of the fourth-century Christian bishop John Chrysostom, excerpted here.

Do you see that demons dwell in their souls and that these demons are more dangerous than the ones of old? . . . Tell me this. Do you not shudder to come into the same place with men possessed, who have so many unclean spirits, who have been reared amid slaughter and bloodshed? Must you share a greeting with them and exchange a bare word? Must you not turn away from them since they are the common disgrace and infection of the whole world? Have they not come to every form of wickedness? . . . What tragedy, what manner of lawlessness have they not eclipsed by their blood-guiltiness? They sacrificed their own sons and daughters to demons. . . . Wild beasts oftentimes lay down their lives and scorn their own safety to protect their young. No necessity forced the Jews when they slew their own children with their own hands to pay honor to the avenging demons, the foes of our life.

Quoted in "John Chrysostom: Eight Homilies Against the Jews," Internet Medieval Sourcebook. www.fordham.edu/halsall/source/chrysostom-jews6.html.

A mosaic portraying St. John Chrysostom is on the walls of the Hagia Sophia in Istanbul.

Religious Hatred and Revenge

took over the apparatus of the Roman state in the fourth and fifth centuries, anti-Semitic acts became commonplace. And the authorities, who were nearly all Christians, did nothing to punish the perpetrators. When a Christian bishop incited a mob to burn down a Jewish synagogue, Ambrose, one of the leading Christian bishops of the late fourth century, asked, "Who cares if a synagogue—home of insanity and unbelief—is destroyed?"[22]

Meanwhile, one of Ambrose's contemporaries, John Chrysostom, who served as bishop of both Antioch and Constantinople, delivered a series of anti-Semitic speeches. "The difference between the Jews and us in not a small one, is it?" John asked. "They crucified the Christ whom you adore as God. Do you see how great the difference is?" Later the same preacher said of the Jews:

> They live for their bellies, they gape for the things of this world, their condition is not better than that of pigs or goats because of their wanton ways and excessive gluttony. They know but one thing: to fill their bellies and be drunk. . . . The synagogue is less deserving of honor than any inn. It is not merely a lodging place for robbers and cheats but also for demons. This is true not only of the synagogues but also of the souls of the Jews.[23]

The anti-Semitic rants of John and other leading Christian clerics not only instigated anti-Semitic violence in that era. After Rome's fall in the fifth and sixth centuries, medieval Christians preserved these hateful writings and used them as excuses to perpetuate violence against Jews. In addition, some Christians circulated horrifying stories about Jews. One common tale was that Jews kidnapped Christian children and killed them in lurid secret religious rituals. Though these stories were patently false, most Christians, whose minds had already been poisoned against Jews, readily believed them. As a result, whenever a Christian child was found dead of unknown causes, suspicions immediately fell on local Jews. In city after city across Europe, in century after century, Jews were periodically and routinely subjected to the "blood libel." Over and over again they were slaughtered, by the dozens, hundreds, or occasionally thousands, to atone for murders they had not committed. Sometimes Jews were killed even when there was no hard evidence of a crime. In Blois, France, in 1171, for instance, a Christian claimed he saw some Jews throw a child's body into a river. No body was ever found and no children had been reported missing. Yet thirty-eight local Jewish leaders were rounded up, locked in a wooden shed, and burned alive.

Host-Nailers, Well-Poisoners, and Flagellants

Another common charge against Jews during the Middle Ages involved the "host," or the wafer that represented the body of Jesus Christ in the Christian sacrament of Holy Communion.

Rumors circulated that Jews sometimes stole the sacred wafers and drove nails through them in an effort to crucify Jesus once again, and that the wafers bled or cried out in pain at the moment they were pierced. Incited to violence by these absurd accusations, Christian mobs periodically attacked the Jewish quarters of cities. In 1298, after a Christian priest in Nuremberg, Germany, claimed that Jews had stolen the host, an angry crowd rushed into the city's Jewish quarter and massacred more than 620 people. That same year, a German knight who believed similar host-nailing stories led a regiment of soldiers in raids on more than 140 Jewish communities; thousand of Jews, including women and children, were butchered without mercy. Even worse was the slaughter in Brussels, Belgium, in 1370. After someone claimed that a Jew had broken a host wafer in half, enraged mobs of Christians annihilated the city's entire Jewish community. Children were dragged through the streets while crowds mutilated their bodies.

Still another false charge leveled against Jews in the medieval centuries was that they poisoned Christian wells

This painting depicts the horrors of the Black Death, which fostered a new wave of anti-Semitism in Europe in the 1300s.

and other water supplies in an effort to achieve revenge on Christians and wipe out Christian communities. One of the earliest reports of this crime occurred in France in 1320. When a disease epidemic of unknown identity struck, a rumor spread that local Jews, Muslims, and lepers had conspired to poison water supplies, thereby causing the sickness.

The charges of well-poisoning against Jews became much more widespread and hysterical only a few years later. In 1347 and 1348, the bubonic plague, which many called the Black Death, struck Europe with catastrophic effects. Millions were infected and died horrible deaths in a frighteningly short period of time. Desperate to find some explanation or assign blame for the catastrophe, many people believed nasty rumors that Jews had poisoned wells across the continent. "Some wretched [Jewish] men were found in possession of certain powders," reported an Italian commentator in April 1348,

> and (whether justly or unjustly, God knows) were accused of poisoning the wells—with the result that anxious men now refuse to drink water from wells. Many were burnt for this and are being burnt daily, for it was ordered that they be punished thus.[24]

And according to the account of a German cleric of the time:

> The persecution of the Jews began in November 1348, and the first outbreak in Germany was at Sölden, where all the Jews were burnt on the strength of a rumor that they had poisoned wells and rivers, as was afterwards confirmed by their own confession. . . . All the Jews between Cologne and Austria were burnt and killed for this crime, young men and maidens and the old along with the rest. And blessed be God who confounded the ungodly who were plotting the extinction of his church. . . . On 20 December in Horw, [the Jews] were burnt in a pit. And when the wood and straw had been consumed, some Jews, both young and old, still remained half alive. The stronger of [the Christians] snatched up cudgels [clubs] and stones and dashed out the brains of those trying to creep out of the fire, and thus compelled those who wanted to escape the fire to descend to hell.[25]

The onset of the Black Death also hurt Jews by creating a new group of anti-Semitic hate-mongers. When prayers to God seemed to have no effect on stopping the spread of the disease, some devout Christians decided that they must go further and demonstrate their devotion by inflicting pain on themselves. Hundreds of these so-called flagellants (from the word flagellate, meaning to punish by whipping) marched from town to town. Reaching a town square, they stripped themselves to the waist and beat themselves with whips, often tipped with metal spikes, until they bled profusely. They cried out, "Spare us, Jesus!," or "Forgive us, blessed Mary!" while they pummeled themselves.

Unfortunately for the Jews, the flagellants did not confine their punishments to themselves. In 1349, in Frankfurt, Germany, a virtual army of flagellants assaulted the local Jewish quarter and massacred hundreds of people. In some other European cities, local dukes and other Christian nobles sent their soldiers to help the flagellants slaughter Jews. In all, European Christians perpetrated at least 350 mass murders of Jews in the span of only three or four years during the great plague. Most of these crimes were documented, sometimes in excruciating detail, and often morally justified as well in eyewitness accounts by Christian writers.

Genocide

Anti-Semitism and religiously motivated attacks on Jews continued in Europe and elsewhere through early modern times and into the twentieth century. The worst atrocity based on hatred of the Jews, or any other religious group for that matter, occurred during World War II. This event was the Holocaust, the attempt by the German Nazis, led by dictator Adolf Hitler, to eradicate the Jews of Europe through systematic genocide. Although Hitler's personal motivation for this orgy of

Thousands Punished for Baby-Killing

Hundreds of mass murders of Jews occurred during medieval times, all of them provoked by blind hatred, ignorance, intolerance, superstition, and false accusations. A large proportion of these incidents involved trumped-up charges of infanticide. In 1255 in Lincoln, England, for instance, the body of an eight-year-old Christian boy was found in the well of a Jewish family. Rumors immediately spread that local Jews had kidnapped the boy, fattened him with milk and bread, and then invited Jews from far and wide to witness his grisly execution by crucifixion. Though these charges were untrue, eighteen Jews were tortured and hanged.

In a 1294 incident in Bern, Switzerland, some Christians claimed that a local Jew had collected several Christian babies in a sack and was eating them one by one. As a result of this preposterous tale, all of the Jews in Bern were either killed or driven away with only the clothes on their backs. And in Trent, Italy, in 1475, almost every Jew in the city was tortured and burned alive after a hysterical charge that they had kidnapped and sacrificed a Christian infant named Simon.

mass murder was mainly racial or ethnic, it was indirectly caused by religious hatred. The Holocaust would not have been possible without the precedent of centuries of religious persecution of Jews by Christians. Haught explains it this way:

> For century after century after century, the Christian church had designated the people to be despised.

The religious believers called the Jews the "Christ-killers," the "enemies of God." . . . When popes ordered Jews to wear [identification] badges and live in ghettos . . . it told the populace that these pariahs [outcasts] were unfit to live among decent folk. . . . Thus, when Adolf Hitler needed a scapegoat group to rally the discontented majority to his cause . . . natural

A pile of human skulls and bones at a death camp in Poland in 1944 stands in mute testimony to the Holocaust.

victims clearly marked by the church were at his disposal. The Christian public, not only in Germany but also throughout Europe, was predisposed to receive the Nazi message of Jew hatred.[26]

Historian Dagobert Runes agrees, pointing out Hitler's historical precedents:

> Everything Hitler did to the Jews, all the horrible, unspeakable misdeeds, had already been done to the smitten people before by the Christian churches. . . . The isolation of the Jews into ghetto camps, the wearing of the yellow spot, the burning of Jewish books and finally, the burning of the people. Hitler learned it all from the church. However, the church burned Jewish women and children alive, while Hitler granted them a quicker death, choking them first with gas.[27]

Indeed, herding naked Jews into gas chambers became the chief method of exterminating them during the Holocaust, although many thousands were shot, starved, or killed by other means. First, Hitler's thugs and secret police herded Jews from across Europe into overcrowded train cars and shipped them to concentration camps, primarily six facilities designed for extermination in occupied Poland. These death camps were equipped with gas chambers. The chambers at the Treblinka camp killed up to two hundred victims at a time. The camp at Auschwitz eventually boasted a gas chamber that could accommodate two *thousand* people at a time. At its height of efficient butchery, Auschwitz murdered some six thousand people per day. In all, nearly 6 million European Jews went to their deaths before the camps were dismantled and Allied forces defeated the Nazis.

Revenge Attacks and Killings in India

Although the Jews have long been the number one target of religiously motivated massacres and hate crimes in Europe and other Western countries, the Far East has also experienced its share of hate and revenge killings. In early modern times, mutual distrust and hatred among Indian Hindus, Muslims, and Sikhs had periodically erupted in violence. Then the British took control of the subcontinent in the 1800s. British authorities managed to keep the peace most of the time among members of these opposing religious groups.

But in 1947, bowing to pressure from many quarters both inside and outside India, the British granted the colony its independence. Many Indians of all walks of life were glad to see the British leave. However, the Hindus and Muslims who were attempting to form a coalition government could not reach mutual agreement and religious tensions rose across the country. Fearing the outbreak of civil war, the British agreed to divide, or partition, the former colony into two new nations—India, which would be ruled by Hindus, and Pakistan, which would be controlled by Muslims.

Though in theory the partition made sense, its actual inception unleashed a torrent of unrest, chaos, and violent conflict. Most Hindus living in the newly created Pakistan abandoned their homes and moved to India. Meanwhile, many Muslims living in India joined a giant mass migration into Pakistan. Much of the Punjab, long the ancestral homeland of the Sikhs, was now part of Pakistan, forcing many Sikhs in that area to leave and make new homes as best as they could in the new India. In an atmosphere of dislocation in which everyone resented everyone else, revenge attacks and killings were inevitable. Rioting, burning, looting, beatings, property seizures, and outright murder became commonplace. Brutal massacres wiped out entire families and even whole villages. Sick, elderly, and handicapped people collapsed along the roads, while cholera, smallpox, and other diseases ravaged the survivors. Even some of these helpless individuals were attacked by angry mobs. In all, between a half-million and a million people died in the violence that accompanied the birth pangs of India and Pakistan.

Perpetuating Hatred

Eventually, the initial violence of partition subsided. But the hatred between Hindus, Muslims, and Sikhs in the region remained palpable, threatening violence at the slightest provocation. At the same time, the new countries of India and Pakistan remained distrustful of each other. Violent incidents continued. The 1984 clash between Hindus and Muslims near Bombay in which 216 died was only one of hundreds of similar incidents. And in 1989, at Indore, in west-central India, Muslims and Hindus fought each other in the streets and set cars afire. At least 15 people were killed and five times that number were wounded. That same year in northern India, a dispute over whether a certain piece of land should house a Hindu temple or a Muslim mosque touched off a riot that killed more than 300 people.

One reason why religious violence occurs decade after decade is that people on each side foster hatred for the other side among new generations of children. Both Indian and Pakistani schoolbooks, for example, twist or even fabricate historical facts, often placing the blame for unrest on members of rival faiths and disparaging their beliefs. One Pakistani text states:

> The Hindus and Muslims . . . kept away from each other. They could not amalgamate in each other's way of life to become one nation. The main reason for this difference of cultures, civilization and outlook was the religion of Islam which . . . is based on the principle of [the] oneness of God. On the other hand, Hinduism is based on the concept of multiple Gods. . . . Islam gives a message of peace and brotherhood. There is no such concept in Hinduism. Moreover Islam preaches . . . equality and justice. It does not differentiate on the basis

A Lone Symbol of Peace and Toleration

Amid all the horrific violence and bloodshed among Hindus and Muslims in India in the 1940s, one man stood out and became a symbol of peace and toleration. He was the world-renowned pacifist and humanitarian Mohandas Gandhi (1869–1948). Widely respected by all Indians, no matter what their religion or background, he frequently brokered truces among the opposing groups by going on hunger strikes. Indeed, respect for Gandhi bordered on reverence and at times his mere presence was enough to temporarily halt the violence. Incredibly, on several occasions during full-scale riots and street battles, he walked calmly right into the fray. Seeing him, the angry combatants, Muslims and Hindus alike, suddenly stopped fighting and allowed him to pass through safely. Only after he had departed did they resume their battle.

Peace activist Mohandas K. Gandhi arrives for a conference with the British prime minister in London in 1931.

Religious Hatred and Revenge

of color, creed, or status. On the other hand, the Hindu society is based on [a] caste system [in which some people are seen to be morally superior to others] which downgrades the entire mankind.[28]

Not all Hindus and Muslims have fallen for these attempts to perpetuate hatred. Asghar Ali Engineer, a politically moderate Muslim scholar and peace advocate, for example, has called for more understanding and reconciliation among Muslims and Hindus. He condemns slanted educational materials on both sides:

> What kind of mindset such books will create among the young students is not difficult to imagine. This is being done to perpetuate eternal enmity between India and Pakistan. India is demonized by Pakistani [textbooks] and Pakistan is demonized by Indian textbooks. It is only peace between the two countries that will be in the interests of the masses of people in both the countries. Such textbooks, should, therefore, be scrapped at the earliest [possible time] and replaced by those which will bring out the strength of composite culture and commonalities between the two countries.[29]

Reason Overcome by Hatred and Rage

Violent disputes between India and Pakistan and between Indian Hindus and Muslims have been paralleled by

A violent Hindu mob overtakes a mosque in India. Religious feuds between Muslims and Hindus have raged for centuries.

The sacred shrine of the Sikhs in India, the Golden Temple, was the scene of deadly religious violence in 1984.

violence involving Sikhs. Sikhism originated in northern India in the 1500s. Like Islam, it posits the existence of a single, all-powerful god; yet like Hinduism, Sikhism embraces the concept of the repeated reincarnation of souls. By far the worst incident of religious hate and revenge in Asia in recent times involved India's Sikh minority. The trouble stemmed from the fact that Sikhism, unlike Christianity, Islam, and most other major religions, is not monolithic, with a single set of precepts, rituals, outlooks, and goals. Rather, Sikhism encompasses progressive, moderate, and conservative fundamentalist factions.

In the early 1980s, a fundamentalist Sikh leader named Jarnail Bhindranwale began advocating Sikh succession from India and the formation of an independent Sikh nation in the Punjab, to be called Khalistan, "land of the pure." When the Indian government refused to consider Bhindranwale's demands, he and his followers preached hatred of Hindus and launched unprovoked attacks on unarmed Hindus, as well as on moderate Sikhs who refused to support

Religious Hatred and Revenge ■ 61

the fundamentalists. Tensions escalated. Then in 1984, Bhindranwale and many of his followers barricaded themselves in Sikhism's holiest shrine, the Golden Temple at Amritsar.

The violence came to a head when India's prime minister, Indira Gandhi, sent troops to free the temple. Nearly a thousand Sikhs, including Bhindranwale, were slain and the temple was damaged, acts that outraged Sikhs everywhere condemned as desecration. Seeking revenge, two of Gandhi's own Sikh bodyguards assassinated her in October 1984. That act, in turn, set off a chain reaction of revenge killings, as thousands of Hindus went on a rampage. As many as five thousand Sikhs, most of them moderates who disapproved of Bhindranwale and his splinter group, were brutally murdered. Some were stabbed or beaten to death, others were doused with kerosene and burned alive. Some moderate Hindus and Sikhs tried to stop the violence. But as has been the case so often throughout recorded history, those seized by hatred and rage inspired by religious zeal were unwilling, or unable, to listen to reason.

Chapter Four

Warfare Among Members of the Same Faith

Members of opposing religious faiths—including Christianity, Judaism, Islam, Hinduism, Sikhism, and many others—have been insulting and fighting one another for many centuries. Yet these violent confrontations have an equally tragic parallel in intolerance, murders, and wars perpetrated between members of the same faith. Internal strife most often stems from disputes over religious doctrine and belief. It is not uncommon, for instance, for one group within a religion to interpret a past event, or a teaching, or a passage from a holy text, differently from another group. To outsiders, these differences can seem subtle, even trivial. Yet to members of that faith they may be extremely significant, and sometimes so divisive that they are worth fighting over.

Consider Catholics and Protestants. Members of both groups are Christians because they worship the same god, accept the divinity of Jesus Christ, and revere the Old and New Testaments (the Bible) as the primary scripture of the faith. Yet the denominations are divided over differences in both belief and practice. Perhaps the most central difference is that Protestants view the Bible as the sole authority for Christian beliefs and in religious disputes. In contrast, Catholics see a number of post-biblical statements and church rules, including directives issued by the popes, as having equal sacred authority with the Bible. Over the centuries, this traditional difference, along with other disputes, has led many Protestants to denounce the popes and to condemn Catholics as papists (a word taken from the term "papal," referring to the popes and their holy office). Horrible massacres and wars between Protestants and Catholics were fought in the 1500s and 1600s, including the debilitating Thirty Years War. Periodic

Warfare Among Members of the Same Faith ■ 63

Bodies lie on the ground in Amman, Jordan, in 2005, victims of terrorism by Muslim suicide bombers.

episodes of bloodshed between the two groups continued into modern times, well into the twentieth century.

Similarly, the history of Islam involves numerous disputes and episodes of violence based on differing beliefs among Muslims. Many, though certainly not all, of these confrontations grew out of the opposing views of Islam's two main subgroups—the Shiites and Sunnis. The Sunnis make up the larger of the two groups, with about 940 million members worldwide at present. They believe that the first four caliphs (supreme leaders of the faithful) who followed the great prophet Muhammad gave rise to the authority of all future Muslim leaders. The Shiites, who number roughly 120 million today, claim this Sunni belief is in error. The Shiites hold that only the descendants and followers of the fourth caliph—Muhammad's son-in-law, Ali—are the legitimate heirs of Muhammad and his teachings. Violence has erupted between Sunnis and Shiites many times over the centuries. Rivalries between the two sects lie at the heart of the sui-

64 ■ Religion and World Conflict

cide bombings and other killings that have occurred in Iraq since the United States invaded that country in 2003.

The Bloody Insurgency in Iraq

The Sunni-versus-Shiite violence in Iraq can be traced in large part to the policies of the former dictator of that nation—Saddam Hussein—and his relations with neighboring Iran. Most of the inhabitants of Iran and Iraq are Muslims. The vast majority of Iranians are Shiites. In Iraq, the population is mixed. About 55 percent of Iraqis are Shiites, while roughly 40 percent of Iraqis are Sunnis and the remaining 5 percent are non-Muslims. Though the Shiites have always been in the majority in Iraq, they have never controlled the government. Both Saddam's predecessors and Saddam himself made sure that the Sunnis held all political power and occupied all important political posts in the country.

Saddam and his Sunni followers did not like the fact that a Shiite-dominated state—Iran—shares a major border with Iraq. But as long as the shah of Iran, a largely secular ruler who enjoyed Western backing, was in charge, Iraq refrained from attacking Iran. In 1979, however, the shah was overthrown by Shiites who instituted a strict theocracy (state ruled by religious leaders and Islamic law). Soon afterward Saddam attacked Iran. A bloody ten-year conflict ensued between Iranian Shiites and Iraqi Sunnis (aided by Iraqi Shiites, who because of ethnic factors felt more allegiance to Iraqi Sunnis than to Iranian Shiites). More than a million people died in the brutal, chaotic fighting. Hoping the Iranian Shiite theocracy would be toppled, U.S. leaders sided with Saddam and supplied him with weapons and other munitions.

Later, however, the Americans felt it necessary to oppose Saddam. In 1991 Saddam invaded the small nation of Kuwait (on Iraq's southeastern border). An international coalition led by the United States drove Saddam's forces out of Kuwait but the dictator's regime survived. Then in 2003 President George

Former dictator of Iraq Saddam Hussein, a Sunni Muslim, addresses his troops in 1987.

W. Bush, assisted by British leaders, ordered an invasion of Iraq intended to remove Saddam from power and establish a democracy in that country. The initial coalition attack succeeded. Saddam and his leading followers were driven from power and many Shiites, seeing that their time to exercise power had finally come, rejoiced. The problem was that the Sunnis were loath to relinquish their traditional power base. Aided by terrorists from other Muslim countries, some of the Sunnis launched an insurrection aimed at driving the Americans out and reinstating Sunni control of the country. That bloody ongoing insurgency claims the lives of hundreds of Iraqis, both Shiites and Sunnis, each month.

Islam's Holiest Sites in Jeopardy

The recent fighting between Shiites and Sunnis in Iraq is certainly not the first example of enmity and bloodshed between these two Islamic sects. Nor is it the first instance of Muslims fighting Muslims regardless of which subgroup of the faith they belong to. Some of the worst such violence in recent times occurred in Saudi Arabia in 1979. Ever since the prophet Muhammad established Islam in the seventh century, the Saudis have been the de facto caretakers of the religion's holiest shrines, located in Mecca and Medina. Every year millions of Muslims travel to Mecca to complete a sacred pilgrimage, or hajj. Among other rituals, they walk seven times around the Kaaba, a sacred cube-shaped monument said to date back to the time of the prophet Abraham.

Because Saudi Arabia houses these and other shrines sacred to Muslims everywhere, Saudi authorities feel obligated to protect the shrines at all costs, even against fellow Muslims. This is what happened in 1979 when a Sunni named Juhaiman al Otaiba, a self-styled new Mahdi, rose up and threatened the integrity of the holy places. According to Haught,

> [Otaiba] was a student of Sheikh Abdel al Baz . . . rector of the University of Medina . . . [who] wrote a paper denouncing the Copernican "heresy" and maintaining that the Sun orbits the Earth. He also said the Earth is flat and that NASA's moon landings were faked. Juhaiman, the new Mahdi, demanded expulsion of all non-Muslims [from Saudi Arabia], abolition of television, and a halt to the education of women.[30]

Hoping to force these and other changes on both Sunnis and Shiites in Saudi Arabia, in November 1979 Otaiba and two hundred of his loyal followers armed themselves with machine guns and took over Mecca's Grand Mosque, which Muslims view as almost as sacred as the Kaaba. The 40,000 or so pilgrims then visiting the shrines were told that

In 2001 thousands of Muslim pilgrims circle around the sacred Kaaba during hajj rituals in Mecca.

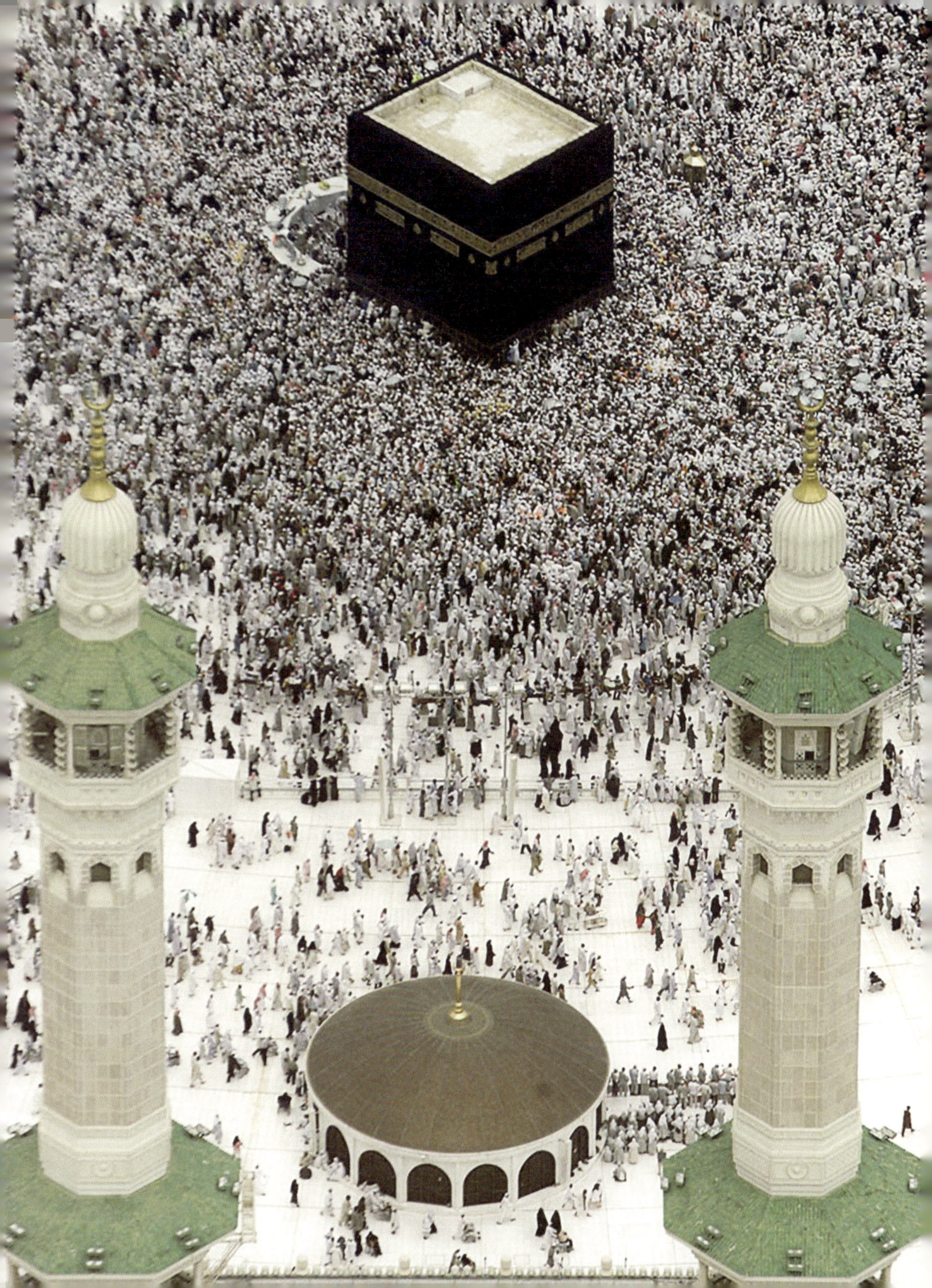

they must join Otaiba's movement or leave the holy site and never return. Otaiba apparently believed he was Islam's new messiah and that Muslims everywhere would flock to his cause. But he was deluded. Five days after he seized the mosque, the Saudi government sent in 2,000 military commandos and nine days of horrific building-to-building and even room-to-room fighting ensued. In the end, 255 people were killed and Otaiba and his leading followers were captured and beheaded.

In addition to the crisis in Mecca, Saudi authorities were forced to deal with an even more destructive confrontation later in 1979. For some time the government had banned a traditional Shiite religious ritual in which worshippers beat themselves, drawing blood, during the holy festival of Ashura (which celebrates the martyrdom of Muhammad's grandson, Hussein). A large number of Shiites decided to defy the ban and performed the ritual. This provoked a response by Saudi police, who moved in to make arrests. In turn, the actions of the police set off deadly riots in which many stores and cars were destroyed and seventeen Shiites were killed. The government then sent in some 20,000 troops, most of them Sunnis. The Sunnis and Shiites came to blows and more people lost their lives.

Persecution of the Baha'i

Although Shiite Muslims have been systematically persecuted or at least politically dominated in Saudi Arabia, Iraq, and other countries, the Shiites have also fought among themselves from time to time. In addition, the Shiites have opposed adherents' attempts to break with tradition, introduce new religious ideas, or form new branches of Shia Islam. The most famous and tragic example of violence sparked by Shiites challenging the basic tenets of Islam is that of the persecution of the Baha'i in the nineteenth and twentieth centuries. The Baha'i began as a branch of Islam and remained a part of that faith for many years. Only later did they come to see their religion as separate from Islam. Today the Baha'i faith is one of the world's fastest-growing religions, with at least 6 million adherents living in more than a hundred countries. Members believe in the existence of a single, all-powerful god and that all people, including women, are equal in God's sight. They also revere the prophets of all the major religions—including Moses, Abraham, Buddha, Muhammad, and Jesus—as various manifestations of God.

For people who routinely preach brotherhood, tolerance, and universal peace, the Baha'i have suffered an inordinate amount of hate, persecution, and violence, especially in the faith's early years. In 1844 an Iranian Shiite holy man proclaimed that he was the Bab, or "gate." By this he meant a portal or medium connecting the ordinary world to the divine world beyond. The Bab claimed that a highly revered ancient preacher, the "Twelfth Imam," spoke to humanity through him. When

Iran Legalizes Anti-Baha'i Persecution

Modern persecutions of the Baha'i in Iran have been sanctioned by Iranian legal authorities. In February 1983 a leading Iranian Shiite judge named Hojjat-ol-Eslam Qazai stated:

The Iranian nation has arisen in accordance with Koranic teachings and by the will of God has determined to establish the government of God on earth. Therefore, it cannot tolerate the perverted Baha'is who are the instruments of Satan and followers of the Devil and the super powers and their agents. It is absolutely certain that in the Islamic Republic of Iran there is no place whatsoever for Baha'is or Baha'ism. Before it is too late the Baha'is should recant Baha'ism, which is condemned by reason and logic. Otherwise, the day will come when the Islamic nation will deal with the Baha'is in accordance with its religious obligation and will.

Quoted in Firuz Kazemzadeh, "The Baha'is in Iran: Twenty Years of Repression," June 22, 2002. http://bahai-library.com/?file=kazemzadeh_bahais_iran_repression.

---

the Bab managed to attract an increasingly large following of Shiite Muslims, the conservative Islamic government of Iran became worried. The authorities eventually arrested the Bab and executed him in 1850.

But to the regret of Iranian leaders, the new branch of Islam the Bab had initiated did not die with him. Two of the Bab's followers, called Bab'is, tried to assassinate Iran's supreme leader, the shah. This act triggered an assault that left some twenty thousand Bab'is dead. Yet the surviving members of the movement persevered. A few years later, one of their number, a man named Baha'ullah, claimed he was a divine messenger. He revitalized the movement, whose members came to call themselves Baha'i after him. Meanwhile, the Baha'i, who by this time no longer viewed themselves as Muslims, spread their faith to Turkey, Cyprus, and other lands.

Back in Iran, the government never gave up persecuting the Baha'i. Many members of the faith were massacred in 1896 and again in 1903, 1906, and 1910. A Baha'i woman who managed to escape and resettle in Canada later recalled:

In 1910 my mother's father and grandfather were first shot in the legs and then hanged because they were Baha'is. Her grandfather did not die immediately, so they put some sticks under his feet, [lit them on fire], and burned him.... Their house was [also] burned.[31]

Warfare Among Members of the Same Faith

Perhaps the worst persecution of Baha'i occurred in Iran in 1955. A conservative Muslim preacher delivered an angry sermon over the radio, calling on all devout Muslims to root out, attack, and destroy the Baha'i, whom he claimed had perverted Islamic teachings. Responding to these hateful words, a mob of soldiers and vigilantes destroyed the main Baha'i temple in the capital, Teheran. At the same time, Baha'i were beaten, raped, and murdered throughout Iran. Only after representatives of the United Nations intervened did the orgy of violence subside. Still more anti-Baha'i persecutions were carried out in Iran and other Muslim nations in the 1960s, 1970s, and 1980s.

The Slaughter of the Huguenots

Fighting and killing among members of the same faith has been a recurring feature of Christianity as well as Islam for many centuries. Some of the worst examples of Christian-versus-Christian violence were wars, battles, and massacres in which Catholics were pitted against Protestants. Although the Thirty Years War, fought between 1618 and 1648, produced the largest single death toll in such hostilities, that conflict was neither the first nor cruelest example of attempts by Catholics and Protestants to wipe each other out.

Indeed, some three generations before the outbreak of the Thirty Years War, some Catholic countries instituted programs designed to rid themselves of Protestants. France and Spain, both predominantly Catholic, signed a treaty in 1559, essentially agreeing to cooperate in harassing and deporting Protestants. What Catholic leaders did not anticipate, however, was the degree to which many Protestants would resist exile. In France alone, eight separate religious wars took place between 1562 and 1589. They are often called the Huguenot Wars, after the French word for Calvinist Protestants, *Huguenots*. Although Catholics committed many atrocities against Huguenots in these conflicts, the Huguenots were frequently equally ruthless and vicious. One Huguenot combatant, for example, made a habit of slaying Catholic priests, slicing off their ears, and wearing a necklace made from the ears. As another Frenchman said in a surviving eyewitness account:

> It would be impossible to tell you what barbarous cruelties were committed by both sides. When the Huguenot is master, he ruins the [Catholic religious] images and demolishes the [Catholic] tombs. On the other hand, the Catholic kills, murders, and drowns all those whom he knows to be of that sect [i.e., the Huguenots], until the river overflows with them.[32]

Perhaps the most infamous incident of the French wars of religion was the so-called St. Bartholomew's Day Massacre of 1572. France's Catholic queen mother, Catherine de Medici, announced that she wanted to make peace with the Huguenots. To that end, she promised her daughter's hand in marriage to a prominent Huguenot leader, Henry of Navarre. Catherine gave safe passage for thousands of Huguenots to travel to Paris for the wedding. But in secret, she also plotted with several Catholic dukes to assassinate a major Huguenot admiral who was scheduled to attend the festivities. The assassin bungled the job, however. Fearing reprisals by the Huguenots, Catherine and the dukes decided to strike first. On the evening of August 24, 1572, a holiday honoring St. Bartholomew, Catholic troops swarmed through Paris's Huguenot neighborhoods, slaughtering men, women, and children. According to one observer:

> Huguenots in Paris were shot, drowned, hanged and butchered by fanatical Catholics. Nowhere were they safe. They were killed in their beds, shot on the rooftops, and

In an example of Christians killing other Christians, Catholics slaughter Huguenots in Paris in the St. Bartholomew's Day Massacre in 1572.

hunted down wherever they sought safety. Women and children were stripped, dragged through the streets, and thrown into the Seine [river]. A basketful of babies was also thrown into the river, and pregnant women had their throats cut.[33]

Similar massacres occurred in other French cities. In all, an estimated seventy thousand Huguenots were butchered in the span of a few days. Their main "crime" had been that they had refused to recognize the pope as their spiritual leader while worshipping Jesus Christ.

Attempts to Eradicate the Anabaptists

The systematic attempts by Catholics to eradicate the Huguenots and other Protestants in the 1500s and 1600s were certainly bloody and cruel. But some historians and religious scholars contend that no single Christian group suffered more at the hands of fellow Christians than the Anabaptists. The Anabaptists made up one of the many Protestant groups that formed in Europe during the eventful sixteenth century. What made them different from the others was that it was not only the Catholics who opposed them and wanted to wipe them out; other Protestants hated the Anabaptists just as much as the Catholics did and were just as eager to destroy them.

The "crime" of the Anabaptists was, once again, a religious difference from other Christians that to most people today seems trivial and not worth fighting over. Yet in the 1500s, that difference was widely viewed as a despicable form of blasphemy against God. One modern expert on medieval Europe explains it this way:

> Membership in [Anabaptist] communities was symbolized by baptism, and . . . infant baptism was vigorously rejected by the Anabaptists. Their name derives from their insistence on adult baptism, following conversion [to the faith], which in practice meant re-baptism, since all Christians of the time had been baptized as infants. . . . [The Anabaptists also rejected] the authority of the state. They declined to take oaths to civil authorities, refused to recognize many laws, and resisted paying taxes. It is not surprising that they seemed to everyone else as dangerous, radical, conspiratorial rebels.[34]

To rid themselves of these allegedly dangerous radicals, other Christians routinely resorted to violence and cruelty. In Switzerland, Anabaptists were rounded up and held underwater until they drowned; to their captors, this punishment seemed appropriate, since the Anabaptists willingly immersed themselves in water (a common form of baptism in those days). In Germany

After seizing the German city of Munster, Anabaptist leaders are tortured and killed by Catholic and Protestant officials in 1536.

72 ■ Religion and World Conflict

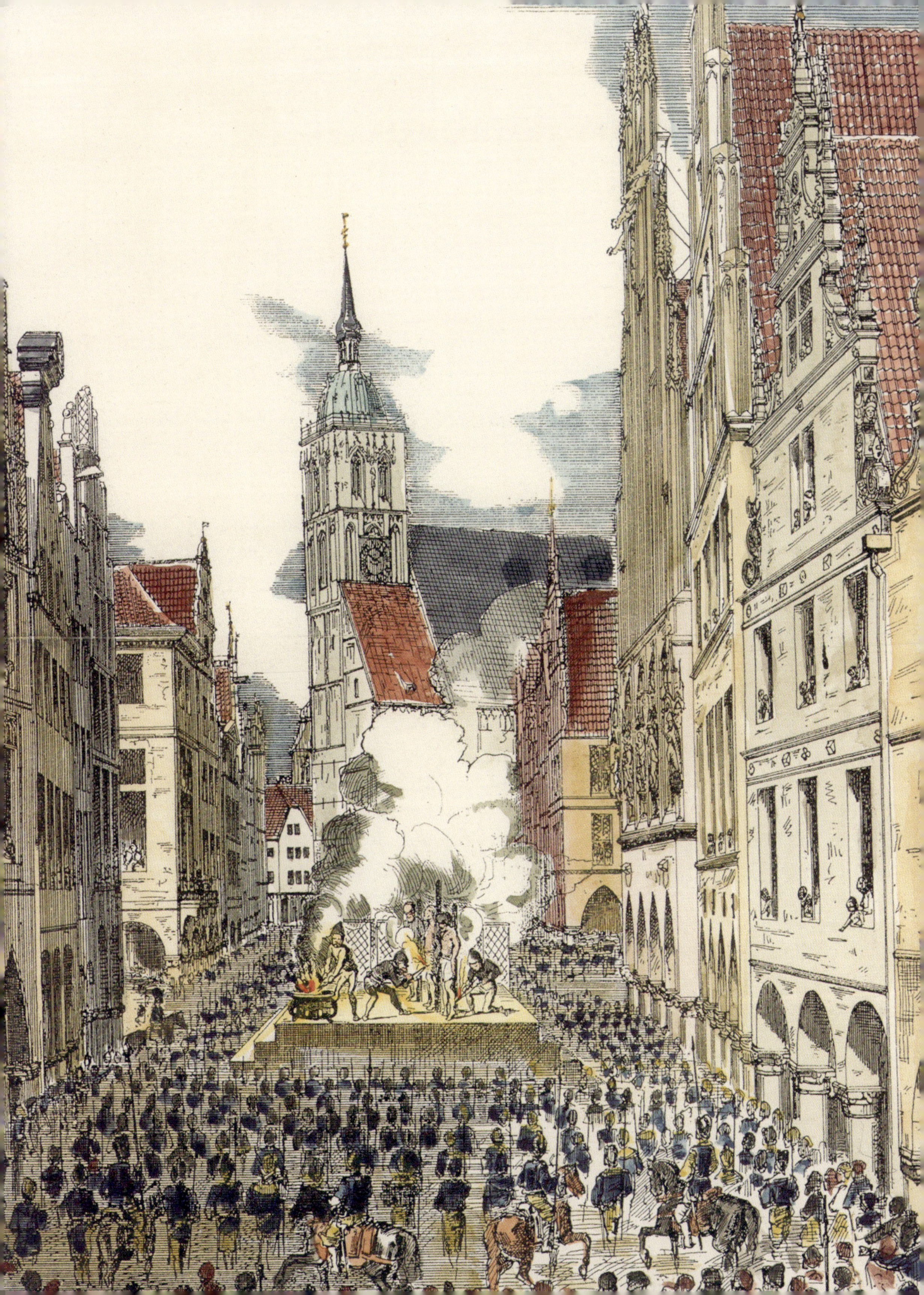

An Anabaptist Explains His Beliefs

Like several other Christian sects, the Anabaptists produced a number of religious documents stating their beliefs and rules. Among these writings was The Seven Articles of Schleitheim, *written mainly by a German Anabaptist named Michael Sattler, who died in anti-Anabaptist violence in 1527. The first of the seven articles deals with the Anabaptists' central issue, adult baptism.*

Observe concerning baptism: Baptism shall be given to all those who have learned repentance and amendment of life, and who believe truly that their sins are taken away by Christ, and to all those who walk in the resurrection of Jesus Christ, and wish to be buried with Him in death, so that they may be resurrected with Him, and to all those who with this significance request it [baptism] of us and demand it for themselves. This excludes all infant baptism, the highest and chief abomination of the pope. In this you have the foundation and testimony of the apostles. . . . This we wish to hold simply, yet firmly and with assurance.

Quoted in J.C. Wenger, trans., "The Schleitheim Confession of Faith." www.bibleviews.com/Schleitheim-JCWenger.html.

---

both Catholics and Protestants attacked local Anabaptists. Even Martin Luther, the founder of the Protestant Reformation and therefore himself a sort of religious rebel, joined in condemning Anabaptists to horrible deaths. Some were drowned, others were burned alive, and still others, including children who had little or no idea of what was happening, were beheaded.

In desperation, in 1534 a group of fleeing Anabaptists seized the German city of Munster. They demanded that all Catholics and Protestants in the city either join them or leave; accordingly, all of the non-Anabaptists departed as quickly as they could. Soon the bishop of Munster arrived with an army and laid siege to the city. After many months of bloody fighting, Munster fell and Catholic soldiers went on a rampage. Anabaptist women were raped, then killed. Meanwhile, the Anabaptist leaders were branded with red-hot irons until all of their flesh had burned away, after which their pitiful remains were placed in cages and hung from a church steeple. The cages and their grisly contents remained in public view as a warning to any would-be Anabaptists for many years. After such horrendous persecutions, one might assume that all of

Europe's Anabaptists were slain. But some did survive; today they make up a number of small Protestant sects, including the Mennonites, Amish, and Hutterians.

Nightmare in Northern Ireland

Even while they were killing Anabaptists, Catholic and Protestant forces in Europe continued to battle each other. At one time or another, such conflicts among fellow Christians took place in every corner of Europe. But one of the worst and most widely publicized trouble spots was northern Ireland. The animosity there between the two main branches of Christianity began in the 1500s when Britain's King Henry VIII broke away from the Roman Church and formed the Protestant Church of England. Henry also forced his new brand of Christianity on Ireland, where at the time the vast majority of people were Catholic. The Irish Catholics resisted and many were killed on both sides. Moreover, similar violent assaults on Irish Catholics continued under Henry's Protestant daughter Elizabeth I (reigned 1558–1603), her Protestant successor, James I (reigned 1603–1625), and the Puritan dictator Oliver Cromwell.

A major turning point in Ireland's history came when James I settled tens of thousands of Protestants in northern Ireland, which became known as Ulster. For generations to come, many Catholics either hid in caves or makeshift villages in the hills or suffered discrimination as low-level workers on

The "Marching Season" Incites Violence

For more than two hundred years, Irish Catholics and Protestants have fought one another over various religious issues and traditions. One Protestant tradition that has consistently raised the ire of Catholics is the so-called marching season. It consists of a series of more than three thousand parades staged by Protestants between Easter Monday and the end of September. One of the biggest and most controversial marches, held on July 12, commemorates the victory of the Protestant English king William of Orange over the Catholics at the Battle of the Boyne in 1690, an event that solidified Protestant power in Ireland. The Protestant marchers say that they are merely celebrating their cultural heritage. But most Irish Catholics view the marches as arrogant, designed to trumpet Protestant superiority over the Catholic minority. As a result, in almost every year during the 1980s and 1990s, the marching season touched off riots, vandalism, and other mayhem in Northern Ireland.

Protestant estates. The division of Catholics and Protestants in Ireland became even more pronounced in 1920, when the British Parliament passed the Government of Ireland Act, which divided Ireland into two separate political units—the predominantly Catholic south and the predominantly Protestant north. Then, in 1949 the south became a nation separate from Britain —the Republic of Ireland.

In Ulster, still part of Britain, meanwhile, the Catholic minority hoped that the north might eventually join with the south, creating a single Irish state. But most of the Protestants of Ulster did not want such a union. And the result was generations of violence between Protestants and Catholics in Ulster. The 1970s witnessed the heaviest bloodshed but the fighting in the 1980s and 1990s was at times almost as bad. "In 1985," for example, a relatively "quiet year," according to Haught, "there were 54 assassinations, 148 bombings, 237 shooting episodes, 916 woundings, 31 knee-cappings . . . and 3.3 tons of explosives and weapons seized—all this in a tiny country with a population of 1.5 million people."[35]

Fortunately for all involved, a truce signed in 1997 is still in force, and people on both sides hope the nightmare of Christians killing and maiming other Christians will not resume. Only time will tell.

Chapter Five

Terrorism in the Name of Religion

The destruction of the World Trade Center towers in New York City in 2001 plunged many countries in the world into what has come to be called the war on terror. The nineteen men who hijacked airplanes and used them as weapons instantly became emblems of terrorism. Terrorism can be generally defined as the commission of kidnappings, bombings, assassinations, mass murders, and other heinous acts designed to strike fear in a general population, either to bring about or to discourage some kind of change.

Indeed, terrorists always have an agenda, even if the agenda is simply to destabilize society. Sometimes that agenda is purely political. For example, in 1972 members of a radical group called Black September infiltrated the Olympic Village in Munich, Germany, took several Israeli athletes hostage, and murdered their captives in a foiled escape attempt. The terrorists' original stated goal, one they never achieved, was the release of two hundred Palestinians then held in Israeli and German jails. Other terrorist acts have been perpetrated to maintain a social or political status quo. This was the case with the Ku Klux Klan (KKK) in the United States (mostly in southern states) in the late 1800s and first half of the twentieth century. During this period Klan members, all whites, committed thousands of beatings, house burnings, and lynchings and other murders against African Americans. The Klan's primary goal was to maintain fear among blacks and thereby perpetuate a racist society in which blacks were treated as inferiors.

What made the September 11 attacks different from the crimes committed by Black September and the KKK was that the nineteen hijackers were all Muslims who were largely motivated by religious extremism. The September 11 terrorists were agents of the Islamic extremist

In Munich in 1972, German politicians meet with a member of Black September in an unsuccessful attempt to negotiate the release of Israeli hostages.

group al Qaeda. That organization's agenda includes driving Western "infidels" out of Muslim countries and establishing Islamic theocracies around the world. In perpetrating terror attacks in New York and Washington in 2001, as well as in Spain and other countries soon afterward, the attackers believed they were acting in God's name and with his approval. And they expected to be rewarded by Allah in paradise.

Although al Qaeda and other similar groups in a sense awakened the modern world to the threat of religiously motivated terrorism, their goals and methods were far from new. People have been committing terrorist acts in the name of one god or another for thousands of years. In fact, "Until the nineteenth century," commentator James Q. Wilson writes for the popular and influential *City Journal*,

> religion was usually the only acceptable justification of terror. It is not hard to understand why. Religion gives its true believers an account of the good life and a way of recognizing evil. If you believe that evil in the form of wrong beliefs and mistaken customs weakens or corrupts a life ordained by God, you are under a profound obligation to combat that evil. If

Religion and World Conflict

you enjoy the companionship of like-minded believers, combating that evil can require that you commit violent, even suicidal, acts.[36]

Significantly, even when some of the goals of such terrorists are political in nature, they justify their violence by claiming that God is on their side.

Killers with Daggers

This was certainly the case with one of the most infamous terrorist organizations in history—the Assassins. Their chief tactic was to kill well-known and powerful military, religious, or national leaders whom they opposed. And their name survives in the common term *assassin*, used to describe someone who slays a well-known public figure.

The Assassins were an extreme offshoot of the Ismailis, one of several Shiite Muslim groups that formed in the centuries immediately following the death of the prophet Muhammad and the spread of Islam throughout the Middle East. Over time, a small group of Ismailis came to view the caliphs and sultans, the Islamic rulers of the large Middle Eastern cities and kingdoms of the day, as too worldly and corrupt. The dissenters held that most of these

A Medieval Christian View of the Assassins

After the Christian king of Jerusalem, Conrad of Montferrat, was slain by an Assassin in 1192, the crusaders became aware of and fascinated by the Assassins' cult. Several Christian writers of that era commented on the Assassins, sometimes conveying accurate information, but just as often passing on rumors and hearsay. One of these writers, Arnold of Lubeck, stated:

This Old Man [of the Mountain, the Syrian Assassins' Grand Master] has by his witchcraft so bemused the men of his country, that they neither worship or believe in any god but himself. Likewise he entices them in a strange manner with such hopes and with promises of such pleasures with eternal enjoyment, that they prefer rather to die than to live. Many of them, when standing on a high wall, will jump off at his nod or command, and shattering their skulls, die a miserable death. The most blessed, so he affirms, are those who shed the blood of men and in revenge for such deeds themselves suffer death.

Quoted in Bernard Lewis, *The Assassins*. New York: Basic, 2003, p. 4.

rulers had abandoned certain basic Islamic principles and therefore must be removed from power. However, the Ismailis who felt this way were relatively few in number. Unable to muster large armies to achieve their aims, they chose instead to form a secretive and deadly organization to terrorize and kill the caliphs and sultans. That organization —the Assassins—began operations in what are now Syria, Iraq, and Iran in the late eleventh century.

The Assassins established several fortresses in remote sites high in mountain ranges, where the armies of the caliphs and other rulers who feared them could not easily find and attack them. The most important and famous of these hideouts was the so-called Eagle's Nest, in the Iranian highlands. The leader of the organization was called the Grand Master. Next in line on the ladder of authority were the Grand Priors, leaders of individual cells of Assassins in various districts of the Middle East. Most of the Assassins fell into a third group—the Propagandists, consisting of soldiers, laborers, servants, and others who carried out the leaders' orders.

Those orders, along with the methods the Assassins employed, followed fairly strict guidelines, which were also set forth by the group's leaders. As Bernard Lewis explains:

> The chosen victims were almost invariably the rulers and leaders of the existing order—monarchs, generals, ministers, major religious [figures]. [The Assassins] attacked only the great and powerful and never harmed ordinary people going about their avocations. Their weapon was almost always the same—the dagger, wielded by the appointed Assassin in person. It is significant that they made virtually no use of such safer weapons as were available to them at the time—the bow and crossbow, missiles [spears and rocks], and poison. . . . The Assassin himself, having struck down the assigned victim, made no attempt to escape, nor was any attempt made to rescue him. On the contrary, to have survived a mission was seen as a disgrace.[37]

Terror Among the Ruling Classes

Following these guidelines, in 1092 the Assassins succeeded in killing the sultan of Baghdad (now in Iraq), Nizam al-Mulk. They also managed to slay other Middle Eastern Muslim leaders in the years that followed, creating widespread terror among the region's ruling classes. In addition, the Assassins occasionally attacked and killed Christian leaders who were trying to dislodge Muslims from the Holy Land during the Crusades. In 1192, for example, one of the Assassins stabbed to death the European nobleman Conrad of Montferrat, who ruled Christian-held Jerusalem at the time.

Yet in spite of such attacks on Muslim and Christian leaders, the Assassins were not above making alliances with key foes to further their own aims. Sometimes Muslim leaders helped the Assassins in hopes of ridding themselves of political or religious rivals. Similarly, Christian crusaders at times made alliances with the Assassins because they had mutual enemies—namely, most Muslim leaders. For a while, one powerful group of crusaders, the Templar knights, had some kind of arrangement with the Syrian Assassins and collected gold and other valuables from them on a regular basis. The purpose of these payments is uncertain. But it may have been to ensure that Christian armies would leave the Assassins' strongholds alone. That allowed the Assassins to concentrate most of their time and energy on stalking and killing Muslim leaders.

For nearly two centuries the Assassins were a potent force in Islamic society and at times seemed almost invincible. But they finally met their match when the Mongols, a nomadic people from central Asia, swept through and conquered the Middle East in the thirteenth century. In 1257 the Mongols, whose warriors were expert horsemen and savage fighters, captured and destroyed the Eagle's Nest after reducing many other Assassin

This page from an illuminated manuscript shows rituals conducted by Assassins, an extremist Muslim sect known for murdering its enemies.

fortresses to rubble. The surviving Assassins begged the Templars and some other leading crusaders to take them in. The Assassins even went so far as to offer to convert to Christianity. But the Christian knights refused to help them and not long afterward a local sultan eradicated the last of the Assassin mountain fortresses in Syria. Even after their demise, however, the Assassins left behind a formidable. frightening, and influential legacy. "Their movement," Lewis points out,

> was regarded as a profound threat to the existing political, social, and religious order.... They did not [ultimately] overthrow that existing order ... yet the undercurrent of messianic hope and revolutionary violence which had impelled them flowed on [in the Middle East], and their ideals and methods found many imitators [in later ages].[38]

India's Sacred Stranglers

Another medieval group, or cult, that killed numerous people and terrorized society in the name of a god utilized strangulation, rather than stabbing, as its signature method of murder. Unlike the Assassins, however, this cult survived and continued to commit crimes well into modern times. These stranglers lived in India and came to be called the Thuggees (from the Hindu word *thag*, meaning "thief," itself derived from a Sanskrit word, *sthaga*, meaning "scoundrel" or "concealed"). It became common to call the Thuggees "thugs" for short. When the British gained control of India in the 1800s, the word *thug*, meaning a violent henchman, entered the English language. The Thuggees came into existence in the 1200s, right about the time that the Assassins were being eradicated by the Mongols. Most Thuggees were Hindus, although a few renegade Muslims and Sikhs supposedly joined the group from time to time.

The standard practice of the Thuggees was for several members—at least ten and often a hundred or more—to lie in wait for travelers on the main roads. They would then pretend to be fellow travelers and gain their victims' confidence by conversing with them and even helping them set up camp and cook meals. Then, one of the Thuggees would give a signal to strike. According to some accounts, the code phrase was "bring the tobacco," although there may well have been other signals. Suddenly, quickly, and with frightening efficiency, the attackers would produce yellow scarves, slip them around their victims' necks, and strangle them to death. Afterwards, it was also standard practice to make away with the victims' valuables.

However, the Thuggees were not ordinary thieves and muggers. They strangled people not simply to rob them, but also as part of what they viewed as a sacred ritual. Originally, they worshipped and killed in the name of Kali, the Hindu goddess of creation, preservation, and destruction. Very little is known about the secret be-

Revered by the Thuggees, Kali, the Hindu goddess of destruction, is typically depicted holding a severed head and sword.

liefs of the cult and how its members justified their actions in the goddess's name. But what seems fairly certain is that they believed they were not committing murder when they killed their victims. Rather, they were offering up their victims to Kali as a kind of sacrifice. According to the Thuggees, Kali desired to maintain a mysterious balance of life on Earth, and she promised that both the stranglers and the victims would receive some kind of reward in the afterlife. Another common belief was that each death carried out by the Thuggees postponed Kali's destruction of the world by a thousand years.

The number of people the Thuggees killed over the centuries is uncertain and regularly debated by scholars. Some place the death toll as high as 2 million; others think this estimate is farfetched and suggest the true toll is likely

Terrorism in the Name of Religion ■ 83

Kali the Destroyer

Kali, the Hindu goddess whom the Thuggees served, is usually portrayed in Indian lore and art as a violent, forceful deity wielding swords in some of her many hands. As pointed out in this description of the goddess in the Web site "Cult of Thuggee," this made her the natural divine mentor of the Thuggee cult.

Kali is the destructive, violent form of the Mother Goddess. . . . Her name is derived from the Hindu word that means "black," and also "time." She is the destroyer of ignorance and wrongdoing, but also creates reality. Her destructive capabilities are not seen as evil but as a necessary aspect of salvation and conversion. . . . In sculptures and paintings, Kali is almost always portrayed in a very ferocious and intimidating manner. . . . Black is the source of all colors and the color that all others go into, so Kali's blackness is a representation of her ability to create and destroy the universe. . . . Her left two hands hold a sword, which is used to cut through ignorance and connections with the worldly, and a severed head, exhibiting her ability to destroy. [These] features are very common in artistic portrayals of the Goddess, and give insight into the violent sacrificial practices of the Thuggees.

Quoted in "Cult of Thuggee." http://shakti.trincoll.edu/~cgiacolo/index.htm.

1 million or fewer. Certainly at the very least the Thuggees long spread a wave of terror through large portions of India. The terrorism and carnage might well have continued indefinitely if the British had not intervened in the 1800s. British military units commanded by Captain William Sleeman rooted out, killed, and arrested many Thuggees. Instrumental in the group's downfall was captured Thuggees' common practice of exposing their compatriots. Ironically, this stemmed from the cult's own beliefs. The Thuggees held that any one of their number who was captured by the authorities was automatically abandoned by Kali. Feeling that he was on his own and would receive no aid from his former comrades, the prisoner usually cooperated with his captors in exchange for lenient treatment. Thus, by about 1890, the long-lived cult of the Thuggees had been exterminated.

Killing Sanctioned by God?

Unfortunately for civilized people everywhere, terrorism perpetrated in the name of religious faith did not die out with the Thuggees. The twentieth century and early years of the twenty-first century have been marred by countless terrorist acts committed by individuals and groups claiming that God inspired or guided them. The great notoriety of the September 11 attacks and other acts of terror carried out by Muslim groups in recent years have given some people the impression that most modern terrorists have been Muslims. But this is a mistaken idea. In truth modern terrorists have belonged to nearly every organized religion, including all branches and sects of Christianity, Islam, Hinduism, Sihkism, Shintoism, and even Judaism, the single most persecuted religion in history.

Believing that God compelled him, Baruch Goldstein (pictured) shot dozens of Muslims in a mosque in Israel in 1994.

For example, sometime in the early 1990s an Israeli named Baruch Goldstein, who hailed from the town of Qiryat Arba, became convinced that the only way to settle the ongoing conflict among Palestinians and Israelis was to terrorize and kill Palestinians. Goldstein believed that God sanctioned any means, even violence, to rid Israel of its enemies. On February 25, 1994, during Islam's holy month of Ramadan, Goldstein entered the Ibrahim Mosque in the town of Hebron, and began firing a machine gun into a crowd of praying Palestinians. Twenty-nine people were killed and 150 were wounded before some of the worshippers subdued the intruder. Most Israelis were shocked and roundly condemned the massacre. But a few of the more radical elements in Israeli society saw Goldstein as a soldier of God and a martyr. These same extremists spoke out against the Israeli government, saying that its efforts to make peace with the Palestinians were a betrayal of Israel and Jews everywhere.

Religious fervor may have inspired a group of Sikh militants to cause one of the most lethal mass murders ever to occur on an airliner. It was also Canada's worst case of mass murder. On June 22, 1985, a bomb planted on Air India flight 182 from Montreal to London exploded over the Atlantic Ocean. The death toll was 329. Police investigators followed a trail of clues that eventually led to several Sikhs who, it was charged, wanted to draw attention to their extreme religious goals. (They were part of a group of Sikhs who, on

Terrorism in the Name of Religion ■ 85

behalf of God, sought to create an independent Sikh homeland inside India.)

Origins of Al Qaeda

Though heinous in their own right, these and many other terrorist acts perpetrated around the world in the past century seem to many people to pale in comparison to the recent death and destruction wrought by al Qaeda. The crimes committed by that organization's operatives began making news in the 1990s. The series of attacks orchestrated by al Qaeda in Africa, Spain, the United States, Britain, Indonesia, and elsewhere have made it the most famous and feared terrorist group in modern history.

Al Qaeda was established by Osama bin Laden, a Saudi who had gone to Afghanistan to fight the Soviets, who had invaded that country in 1979. To understand the roots and goals of al Qaeda, therefore, one must go back to the violence in Soviet-occupied Afghanistan. At the time, the Cold War between the United States and Soviet Union was still ongoing. The United States and Pakistan wanted to help the Afghans drive the Soviets out of Afghanistan. Backed by U.S. and Pakistani funding, a group of Arabs and other Muslims formed an anti-Russian resistance movement whose fighters were called the mujahideen. Bin Ladin, who hailed from a prominent Saudi family that had amassed a fortune in the construction industry, became one of the leading mujahideen. In 1988 he formed and led a subgroup of these fighters that later became known as al Qaeda.

Eventually, Afghanistan proved to be a quagmire for the Soviets, who suffered heavy casualities and withdrew in 1989. At that time, many of the mujahideen, including Bin Laden, decided that they wanted to fight for other causes in which they felt Muslims were being wronged or oppressed. It did not take long for such a situation, in their eyes, to materialize. In 1991 the United States invaded Iraq with the purpose of forcing Iraqi dictator Saddam Hussein to withdraw from Kuwait. Bin Laden and his followers detested Saddam and were all for driving him out of Kuwait. However, they were bitterly opposed to the presence of U.S. troops using Saudi territory from which to launch their attacks on Saddam. Because the Americans were "infidels," Bin Laden said, their presence profaned soil sacred to all Muslims. When Bin Laden publicly opposed his government's policy, the Saudi government revoked his citizenship and expelled him.

Thereafter, Bin Laden and his al Qaeda associates gained an increasing hatred for the United States and other Western countries, convinced that these nations wanted to dominate and subjugate Muslim countries. In both writing and in the media, al Qaeda spokesmen condemned the West, often accusing Americans and others of crimes they never committed. Typical is this statement from the organization's training manual:

Those apostate [unholy] rulers [of Western nations] threw thousands of [Muslim] youths in gloomy jails

Al Qaeda founder Osama Bin Laden sits during an interview in Afghanistan with a Pakistani journalist in 2001.

and detention centers that were equipped with the most modern torture devices and (manned with) experts in the oppression and torture.... The [Western] rulers did not stop there; they started to fragment the essence of the Islamic nation [meaning the worldwide Muslim community] by trying to eradicate its Muslim identity. Thus, they started spreading godless and atheistic views among the youth.[39]

Al Qaeda Attacks the West

At first, al Qaeda based itself in Sudan, whose sympathetic government allowed the organization to thrive there. In 1996, however, responding to mounting pressure from the United States and other Western countries, Sudan ordered Bin Laden and his followers to leave. They quickly made a new base for themselves in Afghanistan, then under a strict Islamic regime controlled by Muslim fundamentalists called the Taliban. In bases located in remote areas of Afghanistan, al Qaeda trained Muslims from around the world in the tactics and ideology of terror.

The purpose of this new army of terrorists soon became clear. In February 1998, Bin Laden and his associate, Ayman al-Zawahiri, issued a fatwa, an Islamic legal decree sanctioned and delivered by religious authorities. It stated in part:

> To kill Americans and their allies, civilians, and military is an individual duty of every Muslim who is able, in any country where this is possible.... By God's leave, we call on every Muslim who believes in God and hopes for reward to obey God's command to kill the Americans and plunder their possessions wherever he finds them and whenever he can.[40]

Not long after these words were released, al Qaeda's terrorist attacks began. In August 1998 its operatives set off bombs in the U.S. embassies in the African countries of Tanzania and Kenya. Some 220 people were killed and more than 4,000 injured in the blasts. Al Qaeda operatives or sympathizers also bombed an American ship, the USS *Cole*, which was then anchored in a harbor in Yemen. Seventeen American sailors died and another 39 were wounded in this attack.

These terrorist attacks put al Qaeda on the map, so to speak, making it clear that the organization was both ruthless and dangerous. However, almost no one was prepared for the horrors wrought by the nineteen hijackers on September 11, 2001. The operation had been carefully planned for years. Several of the hijackers had entered and lived in the United States previously and some had taken flying lessons so that they could pilot the planes after they hijacked them. In all, four commercial passenger airliners were hijacked on September 11. One crashed into the World Trade Center's North Tower at 8:46 A.M.; the second struck the South Tower at 9:02 A.M.; the third plane flew into the Pentagon, in Washington, D.C.,

An Al Qaeda Writing Condemns the West

These are excerpts from the introduction to the original al Qaeda training manual, captured by British law enforcement officials in a raid on a suspected terrorist hideout. Filled with distorted or unsubstantiated information and misleading statements, the manual gives a clear idea of how the organization's leaders poison the minds of recruits about the "evils" of Western, non-Muslim societies.

[At the hands of Western leaders, Muslim] martyrs were killed, women were widowed, children were orphaned, men were handcuffed, women's heads were shaved, harlots' heads were crowned, atrocities were inflicted on the innocent, gifts were given to the wicked, virgins were raped on the prostitution altar. After the fall of our orthodox caliphates on March 3, 1924 . . . our Islamic nation [meaning Muslims living throughout the Middle East] was afflicted with apostate [unholy] rulers [of Western lands] who took over in the Muslim nation. . . . Muslims have endured all kinds of harm, oppression, and torture at their hands. . . . They [the rulers] tried, using every means and [kind of] seduction, to produce a generation of young men that did not know [anything] except what they [the rulers] want, did not say except what they [the rulers] think about, did not live except according to their [the rulers] way. . . . [Then] a large group of those young men who were raised by them [the rulers] woke up from their sleep and returned to Allah, regretting and repenting. . . . [They] realized that Islam is not just performing rituals but a complete system: Religion and government, worship and Jihad (holy war), ethics and dealing with people, and the Koran and sword. Allah's [God's] curse be upon the non-believing leaders and all the apostate Arab rulers who torture, kill, imprison, and torment Muslims.

Quoted in Tom O'Connor, "Religious Terrorism," Mega Links in Criminal Justice. http://faculty.newc.edu/TOConnor/429/429lect13.htm.

at 9:37 A.M.; and the fourth crashed in a southwestern Pennsylvania field at 10:03 A.M., apparently after its passengers tried to subdue the hijackers. At first, Bin Laden lied and claimed that he and al Qaeda had had nothing to do with the carnage on September 11. But later he admitted his involvement. This shocked many Muslims, who had assumed that no responsible member of their faith could perpetrate such ghastly crimes, especially in the name of religion and God. But a number of people around the world, especially historians and others who have studied the human saga and its many wars and atrocities,

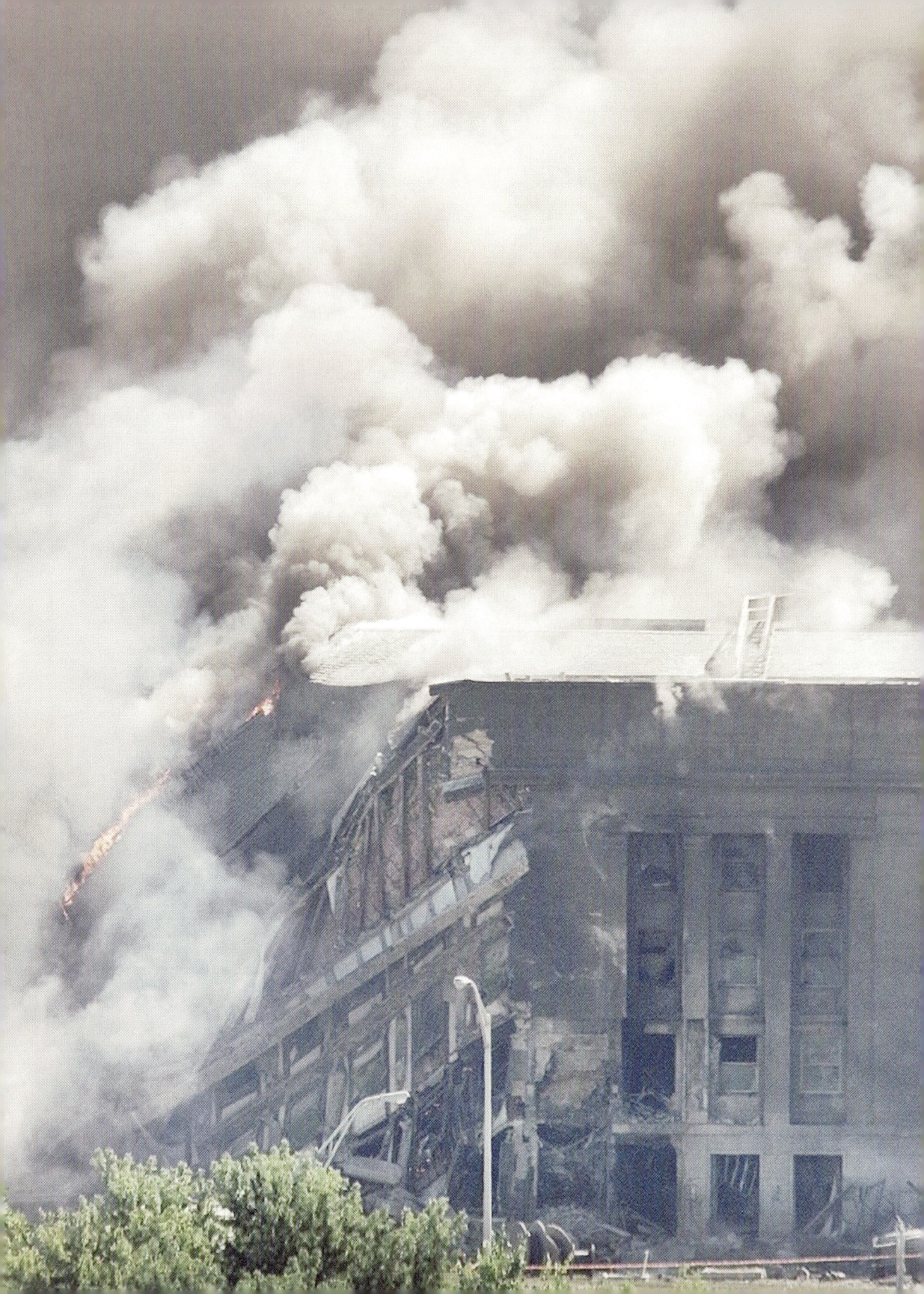

The Pentagon burns after being hit by a hijacked airplane on September 11, 2001.

were not so surprised. They knew that religion, despite its positive achievements and potential for good, has inspired hatred, terrorism, mass murder, wars, and other calamities many times in the past and it will surely do so again in the future. As James Haught sadly and grimly puts it:

> There is plenty of non-religious horror in the world. . . . Many different causes trigger the human instinct for slaughter. Yet it is profoundly depressing that religion—supposedly the cure for human cruelty—often is just another basis for murder and madness.[41]

Notes

Introduction: Killing in God's Name

1. Quoted in James A. Haught, *Holy Horrors*. New York: Prometheus, 1990, pp. iv–v.
2. Haught, *Holy Horrors*, pp. xxi–xxii.
3. Steven Weinberg, interview by Margaret Wertheim, *Faith & Reason*, PBS documentary, September 1998. www.pbs.org/faithandreason/.
4. Koran 47.2–5. Trans. N.J. Dawood. New York: Penguin, 2004, p. 121.
5. Deuteronomy 20:10–14 (Bible, Revised Standard).
6. Steven Weinberg, "A Designer Universe?" *New York Review of Books*, October 21, 1999.

Chapter 1: Warfare Driven by Fundamentalist Beliefs

7. Bonnie G. Smith, ed., *Imperialism: A History in Documents*. New York: Oxford University Press, 2000, p. 37.
8. Quoted in Preetee Brahmbatt, "Who was Mangal Pandey?" Rediff.com India news service, August 10, 2005. http://in.rediff.com/movies/2005/aug/101p.htm.
9. Haught, *Holy Horrors*, p. 138.
10. Bernard Lewis, *The Arabs in History*. New York: Oxford University, 2002, p. 94.
11. William H. McNeill, *The Rise of the West*. Chicago: University of Chicago, 1992, pp. 468, 475.
12. Quoted in Leon Bernard and Theodore B. Hodges, eds., *Readings in European History*. New York: Macmillan, 1958, p. 85.
13. Haught, *Holy Horrors*, p. 76.
14. Quoted in Wilbur C. Abbot, ed., *The Writings and Speeches of Oliver Cromwell*, vol. 2. Cambridge, MA: Harvard University, 1939, p. 127.
15. Quoted in Frederic Harrison, *Oliver Cromwell*. Whitefish, MT: Kessinger, 2004, p. 139.

Chapter 2: Holy Wars for Territory or Political Power

16. Quoted in Norton Downs, ed., *Basic Documents in Medieval History*. Melbourne, FL: Krieger, 1992, pp. 74–75.
17. Quoted in Frederick Duncalf and August C. Krey, eds., *Parallel Source Problems in Medieval History*. New York: Harper and Brothers, 1912, pp. 101–13.

18. Haught, *Holy Horrors*, p. 27.
19. Haught, *Holy Horrors*, p. 19.
20. Christopher Tyerman, *The Crusades*. New York: Oxford University, 2004, p. 139.
21. Quoted in Bernard and Hodges, *Readings in European History*, p. 266.

Chapter 3: Religious Hatred and Revenge

22. Quoted in Paul N. Tobin, "Anti-Semitism," *The Rejection of Pascal's Wager*. www.geocities.com/paulntobin/semite.html.
23. Quoted in "Saint John Chrysostom: Eight Homilies Against the Jews," *Internet Medieval Sourcebook*. www.fordham.edu/halsall/source/chrysostom-jews6.html.
24. Quoted in Rosemary Horrox, ed., *The Black Death*. Manchester, England: Manchester University, 1994, p. 45.
25. Quoted in Horrox, *Black Death*, pp. 208–209.
26. Haught, *Holy Horrors*, pp. 157–58.
27. Quoted in Tobin, "Anti-Semitism."
28. Quoted in Asghar Ali Engineer, "The Pakistani Text Books and Hatred Against India," Institute of Islamic Studies and the Centre for Study of Society and Secularism, January 2000. http://ecumene.org/IIS/csss26.html.
29. Engineer, "The Pakistani Text Books and Hatred Against India."

Chapter 4: Warfare Among Members of the Same Faith

30. Haught, *Holy Horrors*, p. 206.
31. Quoted in Haught, *Holy Horrors*, p. 144.
32. Quoted in Paul N. Tobin, "The Wars of Religion," *The Rejection of Pascal's Wager*. www.geocities.com/paulntobin/war.html#5.
33. Quoted in Brian Bailey, *Massacres: An Account of Crimes Against Humanity*. London: Orion, 1994, p. 30.
34. Neil J. Hackett, *The World of Europe, to 1715*. St. Louis: Forum, 1973, p. 210.
35. Haught, *Holy Horrors*, p. 183.

Chapter 5: Terrorism in the Name of Religion

36. James Q. Wilson, "What Makes a Terrorist?" *City Journal*, Winter 2004. www.city-journal.org/html/141whatmakesaterrorist.html.
37. Bernard Lewis, *The Assassins*. New York: Basic, 2003, pp. xi–xii.
38. Lewis, *Assassins*, pp 139–40.
39. Quoted in Tom O'Connor, "Religious Terrorism," MegaLinks in Criminal Justice. http://faculty.ncwc.edu/TOConnor/429/429lect13.htm.
40. Quoted in Haught, *Holy Horrors*, p. xii.
41. Haught, *Holy Horrors*, p. 225.

For Further Reading

Books

Christon I. Archer et al. *World History of Warfare*. Lincoln: University of Nebraska, 2002. A comprehensive, well-informed overview of warfare through the ages.

Patrick Brogan, *The Fighting Never Stopped: A Comprehensive Guide to World Conflict Since 1945*. New York: Vintage, 1990. Covers not only the major wars of the period, but also local conflicts, many of which were fought over religious differences or disputes.

George Friedman and Meredith Friedman, *The Future of War: Power, Technology, and American World Dominance in the Twenty-First Century*. New York: St. Martin's Griffin, 1996. Focuses on the changing strategies of warfare in the twentieth century and how countries, as well as terrorists, will fight wars in the foreseeable future.

Thomas L. Friedman, *Longitudes and Latitudes: The World in the Age of Terrorism*. New York: Anchor, 2003. An excellent commentary on the reasons for Muslim hatred of the West and the advent of world terrorism.

James A. Haught, *Holy Horrors*. New York: Prometheus, 1990. An excellent, readable overview of most of the wars, murders, and witch hunts that have been motivated by extreme religious devotion.

John Keegan, *A History of Warfare*. New York: Random House, 1993. One of the leading scholars of the subject explains how the major world conflicts came about and how they were fought.

Andrew Langley, *September 11: Attack on America*. Mankato, MN: Compass Point, 2006. A good, brief, and easy-to-read synopsis of the terrifying assaults on New York and Washington, D.C.

Bernard Lewis, *The Assassins*. New York: Basic, 2003. One of the world's leading scholars of Islam traces the rise and fall of this radical medieval Islamic sect.

Barnet Litvenoff, *The Burning Bush: Anti-Semitism and World History*. New York: E.P. Dutton, 1988. This eye-opening overview of the subject covers numerous historical examples of anti-Jewish hatred and persecution.

Joseph Perez, *The Spanish Inquisition*. New Haven, CT: Yale University, 2005. The comprehensive study of the operation and abuses of the Inquisition over the course of some 350 years.

Regine Pernoud, *Joan of Arc: Her Story*. New York: Macmillan, 1999. A wonderful, moving study of the great Christian martyr, including her trial and execution by representatives of the Inquisition. Pernoud is one of the leading modern scholars of Joan.

Christopher Tyerman, *The Crusades*. New York: Oxford University, 2004. A brief but informative overview of the Crusades by one of the foremost historians of that era.

Web Sites

Anti-Semitism and Responses (www.jewishvirtuallibrary.org/jsource/antisem.html). A collection of short articles about the history of anti-Semitism and how some people have tried to fight against it.

The Crusades, Internet Medieval Sourcebook (www.fordham.edu/halsall/sbook1k.html). A fulsome and very useful collection of both medieval and modern sources about the Crusades.

The 9/11 Attacks: September 11 Digital Archive (www.911digitalarchive.org). A still-growing collection of photos, audio recordings, news commentaries, and other forms of documentation of the September 11 attacks.

Index

Afghanistan, 86, 88
African Americans, 77
airplane bombings, 85–86
airplane hijackings, 12–13, 88–89
Amin, al-, 23
Amish, 75
Anabaptists, 72, 74–75
Anglican Church, 30
Anson, George, 21
anti-Semitism, 49–55
Arnold of Lubeck, 79
Ashura, 68
Ashur (Assyrian god), 35
Assassins, the, 79–82
Assyria, 35
Auschwitz, 57
Austria, 54

Bab, the, 68–69
Baha'i, 68–70
Baha'ullah, 69
baptism, age at, 72, 73
Base, the. See al Qaeda
Belgium, 53
Bhindranwale, Jarnail, 61–62
Bible, 18, 63
bin Laden, Osama, 16, 86
Black Death, 54
blood libels, 52
Britain
    Christian-versus-Jewish violence, 55
    India and
        partition, 57–58
        Sepoy Mutiny, 20–23
        Thuggees, 84
    Ireland and, 75–76
    Puritans, 30–31, 33–35
    Sudan and, 46–47
bubonic plague, 54
Burgundians (Germanic tribe), 25–27
Bush, George W., 41, 65–66

Canada, 85–86
Catholic League, 42
Catholics
    Bible and, 63
    Huguenots and, 70–72
    Puritans and, 30, 33

Charles I (king of England), 33
Chevalier de la Barre, Jean-François, 19
Christianity
    fundamentalism
        in France, 19–20
        Puritans, 30–31, 33–35
    Roman Empire and, 35, 48, 50, 52
Christian-versus-Christian violence
    basis, 63
    Ireland, 75–76
    Puritans, 30–31, 33–35
    slaughter of Huguenots in France, 70–72
    Thirty Years War, 36, 41–44

violence against Anabaptists, 72, 74–75
witch hunts, 27–28, 30
Christian-versus-Jewish violence
   during Middle Ages, 41, 49–55
   Nazi genocide, 55–57
   during Roman Empire, 50, 52
Christian-versus-Muslim violence, 16, 37–39, 41, 49
Christ-killers charge, 50, 52, 56
Chrysostom, John, 51, 52
Church of England, 30, 75
City Journal, 78–79
Cold War, 86
concentration camps, 57
Conrad of Montferrat (Christian king of Jerusalem), 79, 80
Constantine (Roman emperor), 35
Cromwell, Oliver, 16, 31, 33–34, 35
Crusades, 37–39, 41
   Assassins and, 79, 80–81
   justification for, 16
   slaughter of Jews, 49

Darfur (Sudan), 47
death camps, 57
Deus vult (God wills it), 37
Drogheda (Ireland), 31, 33

Eagle's Nest, 80, 81
Eckford (British officer in India), 21
Egypt, 46
Enfield P/53 rifles, 21
Engineer, Asghar Ali, 60
"enlightened one," 46
Europe
   Muslims in, 25–27
   Thirty Years War, 36, 41–44
   witch hunts, 27–28, 30
   see also specific nations

fatwas, 88
Ferdinand II (German prince), 42
First Crusade, 37
flagellants, 54–55
Foundation, the. *See* al Qaeda
France
   Christian fundamentalism, 19–20
   Christian violence against Jews, 52
   Muslim invasion, 25–27
   slaughter of Huguenots, 70–72
   Thirty Years War and, 44
Franks (Germanic tribe), 25–27
fundamentalism
   Christian, 19–20
      Inquisition, 27–28, 30
      Puritans, 30–31, 33–35
   Muslim
      in India, 20–23
      al Qaeda, 12–13, 78, 86, 88–89
      in Saudi Arabia, 66, 68
   Sikh, 61–62

Gabriel (angel), 23
Gandhi, Indira, 62
Gandhi, Mohandas, 59
gas chambers, 57
genocide, 55–57
Germany
   Christian violence against Jews, 53, 54, 55
   Nazi genocide, 55–57
   Palestinian murder of Israelis, 77
   Thirty Years War, 36, 41–44
   violence against Anabaptists, 72, 74–75
Ghafiqi, 'Abd ar-Rahnan al, 25–27
ghettos, 56, 57
Golden Temple (Amritsar, India), 62
Goldstein, Baruch, 85
Gordon, Charles George, 46

Government of Ireland Act (1920), 76
Granada (Spain), 27
Gurkhas, 22–23

Haught, James A.
   on Nazi genocide, 56
   on Crusades, 39, 41
   on witch hunts, 30
   on Otaiba, 66
   on religion and violence, 14, 91
   on Sepoy Mutiny, 22
   on violence in Ulster, 76
Henry of Navarre, 71
Henry VIII (king of England), 30, 75
heresy, 27–28, 30
Hindus
   Sikh violence against, 61–62
   Thuggees, 82–84
Hindu-versus-Muslim violence
   education and, 58, 60
   India, 20, 48, 57–58
Hindu-versus-West violence, 20–23
Hitler, Adolf, 55–57
Holocaust, 55–57
Holy Inquisition, 27–28, 30
holy wars
   characteristics of, 15–16, 18
   political motives for
      Crusades, 16, 37–39, 41
      Puritans, 30–31, 33–34
      Thirty Years War, 36, 41–44
host-nailers, 52–53
Huguenots, 70–72
Hussein, Saddam, 65–66, 86
Hutterites, 75

India, 20
   British partition, 57–58
   Sepoy Mutiny, 20–23
   Sikh violence, 61–62

Thuggees, 82–84
Innocent VIII (pope), 28
Inquisition, 27–28, 30
Iran, 65, 69–70
Iraq
   American invasion of, 41
   invasion of Kuwait, 86
   Muslim-versus-Muslim violence, 65–66
Ireland
   Christian-versus-Christian violence, 75–76
   Puritans, 31, 33–35
Ironsides, 33
Islam, 23–27, 66, 68
   see also headings beginning with Muslim(s)
Ismailis, 79–80
Israel
   Olympic Games murders and, 77
   Palestinian suicide bombers, 44, 46
   territory and Palestinians, 36
   violence against Palestinians, 85
Italy, 55

James I (king of England), 75
Jerusalem, Crusades and, 37, 39
Jesus Christ, 49–50
Jews
   Christian violence against
      during Middle Ages, 41, 49–55
      Nazi genocide, 55–57
   Muslim violence against
      murder of Olympic athletes, 77
      Palestinian suicide bombers, 36, 44, 46
   violence against Palestinians, 85
jihad, 16, 23–27

Kaaba (Mecca, Saudi Arabia), 66, 68

Kali (Hindu goddess), 82, 83, 84
Kenya, 88
Khalistan, 61
Khartoum (Sudan), 46
Koran
    basis, 23
    importance, 24–25
    justification for violence in, 16
Ku Klux Klan (KKK), 77
Kuwait, 65, 86

lands overseas, 39
Lewis, Bernard, 24, 80, 82
Lord Protector, 33
Luther, Martin, 74

Magdeburg (Germany), 43–44
Mahdi, the, 46
Malleus Maleficarum (Witches' Hammer), 28, 30
marching season, 75
Martel, Charles, 25–27
Massachusetts Bay Colony, 30
Maxentius, 35
McNeill, William H., 25
Mecca (Saudi Arabia), 23, 66, 68
Medici, Catherine de, 70–71
Medina (Saudi Arabia), 23, 66, 68
Mennonites, 75
Milvian Bridge, Battle of, 35
Mongols, 81
Moradabad (India), 20
Muhammad, 23, 64
Muhammad Ahmad, 46
mujahideen, 86, 88
Mulk, Nizam al-, 80
Munster (Germany), 74–75
Muslims
    Christian-versus-Muslim violence, 16, 37–39, 41
    Shiite versus Sunni violence, 64–65
    see also Islam
Muslim-versus-Baha'i violence, 68–70
Muslim-versus-Christian violence
    Assassins, 79, 80
    eighth century Europe, 25–27
    Sudan, 37, 46–47
Muslim-versus-Hindu violence
    education and, 58, 60
    India, 20, 48, 57–58
Muslim-versus-Jewish violence
    murder of Olympic athletes, 77
    Palestinian suicide bombers, 36, 44, 46
Muslim-versus-Muslim violence
    Assassins, 79–82
    Iraq, 65–66
    Saudi Arabia, 66, 68
Muslim-versus-West violence, 86
    Sepoy Mutiny in India, 20–23
    September 11, 2001 attacks, 12–13
    goals, 15, 77–78, 88–89
    salvation as reward, 16

Nazis, 55–57
Nero (Roman emperor), 48
New York City, 12–13
Nimeiry, Gaafar Muhammad al-, 47
9/11 attacks. *See* September 11, 2001 attacks
Northern Ireland, 75–76

Olympic Games, 77
Omar I (caliph), 23
Otaiba, Juhaiman al, 66, 68
Outremer, 39

pagans, 48
Pakistan, 57–58

Palestinian Arabs
 Jewish violence against, 85
 murder of Israeli athletes, 77
 as suicide bombers, 44, 46
 territory and Israel, 36
Pennsylvania, 12–13, 89
Pentagon, 12–13
Peter the Hermit, 37
Prophet, the. *See* Muhammad
Protestant Reformation, 30
Protestants, Bible and, 63
Protestant Union, 42
Punjab, 58, 61
Puritans, 30–31, 33–35

al Qaeda, 12–13, 78, 86, 88–89
Qazai, Hojjat-ol-Eslam, 69

Republic of Ireland, 76
Restoration, 34
Roman Empire, Christianity and, 35, 48, 50, 52
Runes, Dagobert, 57

Salem (Massachusetts Bay Colony), 30
Satan, 27–28
Sattler, Michael, 74
Saudi Arabia, 23, 66, 68
Seljuk Turks, 37
Sepoy Mutiny, 20–23
September 11, 2001 attacks, 12–13
 goals, 15, 77–78, 88–89
 salvation as reward, 16
Seven Articles of Schleitheim, 74
Shiite Muslims, 64–65, 79
Sikhs
 ancestral homeland, 58
 Sepoy Mutiny and, 22–23
 violence against Hindus, 61–62
 violence by, 85–86

Sleeman, William, 84
Smith, Bonnie G., 21
Soviet Union, 86
Spain
 Christian conquest, 27
 Huguenots, 70
 Thirty Years War and, 44
 St. Bartholomew's Day Massacre (1572), 70–72
stranglers, 82–84
Sudan, 37, 46–47
suicide bombers, 36, 44, 46
Sunni Muslims, 64–65
Switzerland
 Christian-versus-Jewish violence, 55
 violence against Anabaptists, 72
 witch hunts, 30

Taliban, 88
Tanzania, 88
Templar knights, 81, 82
terrorists
 agenda, 77–79
 airplane bombing, 85–86
 Olympic Games attack, 77
 September 11, 2001 attacks, 12–13
 goals, 15, 77–78, 88–89
 salvation as reward, 16
 suicide bombers, 36, 44, 46
Thirty Years War, 36, 41–44
Thuggees, 82–84
Tours, Battle of, 26–27
Treblinka, 57
Twelfth Imam, 68
Tyerman, Christopher, 41

Ulster, 75–76
Umar I (caliph), 23
United States, 41, 65–66, 86, 88

see also September 11, 2001 attacks
United States Constitution, 44
Urban II (pope), 37, 38
USS *Cole*, 88

violence and religion
   characteristics of, 15–16, 18, 83
   enigma of, 14–15
   hate-revenge pretext for, 48–52
   political motives for
      Israel, 36
   Puritans, 30–31, 33–34
   Sudan, 37, 46–47

see also holy wars
Voltaire, 19

Washington, D.C., 12–13
well-poisoners, 53–54
Westphalia, Treaty of, 44
Wilson, James Q., 78–79
Witches' Hammer, 28, 30
witch hunts, 27–28, 30
World Trade Center, 12–13
Worms (Germany), 41

Zawahiri, Ayman al-, 88

Picture Credits

Cover, Saprizal/UPI/Landov
akg-images, 22, 29, 43, 73, 81
akg-images/British Museum, 50
akg-images/Cameraphoto, 53
akg-images/Joseph Martin, 38
The Art Archive/Academia BB AA S Fernando Madrid, 28
The Art Archive/Dagli Orti, 26
The Art Archive/Gordon Boy's School, Woking/Eileen Tweedy, 45
Erich Lessing/Art Resource, N.Y., 49
Victoria and Albert Museum, London/Art Resource, N.Y.,83
Associated Press, AP, 85
Bridgeman Art Library, 36
© Archivo Iconografico, S.A./CORBIS, 10 (lower), 10 (upper right)
© Krause Johansen/Archivo Icongrafico,S.A./CORBIS, 71
© Sean Adair/Reuters/CORBIS, 11 (lower right)
© Bettmann/CORBIS, 11 (lower left), 78
© Bennett, Dean;Eye Ubiqutous/CORBIS, 61
© Maurizio Gambarini/dpa/CORBIS, 10 (upper Left)
© Roger Ressmeyer/CORBIS, 11 (upper left)
© Reuters/CORBIS, 14-15, 87, 90
 Leonardo de Silva/CORBIS, 40
© Sygma/CORBIS, 65
Getty Images, 60
AFP/Getty Images, 13, 56
Marvin Naamani/AFP/CORBIS, 67
Hulton Archive/Getty Images, 20, 42, 59
Time Life Pictures/Getty Images, 32, 51
Majed Jaber/Reuters/Landov, 64
Mary Evans Picture Library, 31

About the Author

Ted Hodges majored in history in college and has travelled to and studied in more than twenty foreign countries. He has also written several books and articles about warfare, including religious conflicts around the world. Mr. Hodges lives in Minnesota with his wife Mary.